The Living

European Women Writers Series

Pascale Kramer

The Living

(Les Vivants)

Translated by Tamsin Black

UNIVERSITY OF NEBRASKA PRESS : LINCOLN AND LONDON

NATIONAL
ENDOWMENT
FOR THE ARTS
A great nation
deserves great art.

Publication of this book was assisted by a grant
from the National Endowment for the Arts. *Les
Vivants* © Calmann-Lévy, 2000 ¶ English trans-
lation © 2007 by the Board of Regents of the University of Nebraska ¶ All rights reserved ¶ Man-
ufactured in the United States of America ¶ ∞ ¶
Library of Congress Cataloging-in-Publication
Data ¶ Kramer, Pascale, 1961– ¶ [Vivants. Eng-
lish] ¶ The living = Les vivants / Pascale Kramer; translated by Tamsin Black. ¶ p. cm. —
(European women writers series) ¶ ISBN-13:
978-0-8032-2774-3 (cloth: alk. paper) ¶ ISBN-13: 978-
0-8032-7823-3 (pbk.: alk. paper) ¶ I. Black, Tamsin. II. Title. III. Title: Vivants. ¶ PQ2671.R287V5813
2007 ¶ 843'.914-dc22 ¶ 2006030915 ¶ Designed and
set in Monotype Dante by R. W. Boeche.

The Living

L ouise was coming to spend a few days at home with Vincent and their two children. Benoît was waiting for them, leaning shirtless out of his bedroom window, half-asleep and dazzled by the midday sun on the stretch of main road that separated the house from the first apartment blocks of S. It was the 8th of May, very empty and lovely on the crisscross of plowed fields all around. Benoît had been up late the night before, and his tongue was rough with an aftertaste of rusty iron. On the parking lot below, the uprooted pumps of his father's old service station gave off an already forgotten smell of gasoline. Benoît let fall a mouthful of spit, and it splattered on the tarmac in a star shape. There was no sound, just the tremble of the dwarfed meadow shunted against the side of the house and that exhilarating, pure, holiday stillness. When he looked up, the car's red roof was emerging from the edge of the landscape. Louise's bare arm was held out to the breeze and long strands of her hair were blowing through the open window. A chunky plastic ring on her finger shot orange rays into the spring air. Benoît guessed she was humming; he was infinitely pleased to see her.

Vincent made a wide curve and pulled up in the shade of the housefront. Louise was wearing dark glasses and Benoît saw the sky and house pass across them when she leaned out to blow him a kiss. Her fleshy lips showed only a trace of makeup and lent a sort of violence to the placid perfection of her face; she put her forefinger on them and pointed to the two children who were asleep in the back. Beside her, Vincent had not even raised his eyes to the window. He was tidying the pile of cassettes on the dashboard; Benoît guessed from the expression of his angular profile, a cigarette stuck in his mouth, that he was annoyed with Louise. Arguments were part of the aggravation she took in her stride with incredible good nature. She had knelt on her seat to watch the children sleeping; Vincent emptied the ashtray out of the door and must have finally said something to her, for she sat back on her heels to listen, leaning her head against the seatback and playing with the orange ring in the lap of her miniskirt. Benoît rested his chin on the sun-warmed concrete of his window; the midday warmth was making his armpits damp. He found it pleasant to make the moment of waking last while he admired his sister's infinite patience.

The weather had been fine for only a few days, and a watery blue sky was still trailing long skeins of cloud that suddenly cast a chill over the countryside. Louise in her beach T-shirt with its low-cut back and shoulders made him cold. She had pushed her door open to brush her hair and was looking indulgently at the dirty white housefront, decorated, as though by chance, with a handful of purple petunias. Benoît realized that she had not been back for nearly a year and that he had gotten used to it.

Vincent got out to take a leak against the heap of scrap metal and tangle of weeds beside the shed; he shouted to Louise that he had things to do in town and she merely waved her brush over the car hood in reply. He went off, doing up his belt over his shirt, which the wind was distending like a sail. His steps rang for a long time on the highway, so strangely deserted in this fine weather. Louise got out of the car—the thick soles of her sandals made her look even lankier—and stretched in the sun, smiling at her brother, Vincent's ill humor already forgotten. Benoît could see the knot of her belly button yawning in the taut skin of her stomach under the waistband of her skirt; he had not remembered that she was so pretty.

Louise opened one of the rear doors partway to give the children some air, then put a great travel bag on the hood and took out a series of neatly folded clothes. She stood very straight, and as she put her hair back, her shoulders rippled in a move that was unconsciously provocative. Louise was gorgeous without being flirtatious. At nearly twenty-five, and despite two already big children, she still had the air of a schoolgirl to which her wide, finely chiseled jaw and short flat nose added an untamed charm. Benoît thought about going down to join her but did not find the courage to shake off his somnolence. A smell of fatty roasting meat floated up the stairs. He could hear his mother moving the kitchen stools about, striking the broom roughly against the baseboards the way she did when she was tired. The rare visits from this accidental little family revived old irritations she had never thrown off. She did not like Vincent; she could not forgive him for having gotten Louise pregnant at sixteen, partly to get himself talked about in the neighborhood. That her daughter was radiantly happy anyway offended her common sense; she had never made any secret of the fact that she had hoped to the end that the baby would not survive, nor later that she had never managed to love the children completely, without resentment.

A light breeze blew the car door closed with a bang, disturbing the children's sleep. Louise watched them toss restlessly, bewildered by the heat and unfamiliar surroundings, then she went to open the door for Fabien, who slipped into her arms as limp as a little invalid. He would be eight in two days' time, which his narrow face and girlish lips belied. After wiping his cheek with the bottom of her T-shirt, Louise sent him off for a pee against the shed wall, then turned to the second one, Luc, whom she dug out of the car, still half-asleep from the ride. She hugged him to her just as she had petted the older boy, then she smoothed his hair with the flat of her hand and put a white shirt on him that seemed to hurt his eyes. Benoît had always seen her like this with her children: adorably, almost annoyingly, loving. He pitied them for these effusive outbursts, which had been his joy and terror when he was small and she used to come into bed with him to make him promise, without moving or opening his eyes, to love her forever and enough to run away from home with her one day. She must think her role as a mother too serious for such silliness—she performed it like a rite. Far too nice to bring them up, she let them grow up, showering them with gifts, new clothes, and ceremonious kisses. She had turned out two timorous kids who were loved for their good looks and listlessness. They made little noise and few demands for attention. Benoît hardly knew them, Louise having moved to the south with Vincent's family when she was expecting the second one; he had taught them to ride a bike and taken them to eat ice cream, but there was scant satisfaction to be gained from entertaining them.

Benoît pulled yesterday's clothes over his unwashed body; the discomfort was at once pleasant and depressing. Downstairs, his mother was shouting to Louise to make up the beds, and wail followed wail from the children in the garden. As he brought his head through his shirt, Benoît spotted Vincent coming back along the road. He was tall and a bit round-shouldered, and he walked with a shrugging movement that jolted his shock of dark hair. He must have gone to have a beer or buy cigarettes. Benoît knew he was annoyed at having to come here, as though vexed with them for the lack of satisfaction his marriage to the prettiest girl at school had brought him. All that remained of his brief and probably fortuitous love life was the feeling that he had let himself be had. Despite his taciturn nature and fits of anger, Louise had stayed even-tempered toward him. She would most likely have been surprised if anyone had asked her if she loved him.

Benoît heard Louise dragging her travel bag from stair to stair. The sun was spreading over his unmade bed and the room was full of light; when Louise came in she looked as blond as a Barbie to him. She pressed her cheek to his — Benoît guessed she had her eyes closed — then sat down on the edge of the bed, tugging unconsciously at the sheets and laughing at the chaos. Electricity from the bedcovers made her hair stand out in spikes about her shoulders. She was smiling, her chin in the crook of her hands and her elbows planted on her thighs, as elegantly tangled as a fawn. Benoît caught the fruity waft of her chewing gum; her face, so close to his, was as smooth as a fruit. After making him swear not to tell anyone, she half lay down on the bed and took out of her tiny skirt pocket a note folded in eight. Each time she came she gave him one or two hundred francs stolen from Vincent's mother; it was her way of sharing what she believed to be the happiness of her marriage: a big, new house with televisions in the bedrooms and one whole floor for the use of the young couple. Louise had kept Benoît's hand in hers; the note seemed to wilt between their two palms. She described how she had argued with Vincent before leaving and showed the little scratch he had given her under her ear by pulling her hair. There was no bitterness in what she said; Louise made no particular demands of love and readily put up with the exasperations of conjugal life. Benoît did not know how to reply, in thrall to the seductive sound of her slow voice. She was silent, her pale eyes devotedly searching the face of this seventeen-year-old brother whom she thought handsome and kind; the sun gave her eyes the complicated depth of glass marbles. Benoît wanted her to stay a bit longer, but the children were already starting to fret that she was out of sight. So Louise stood up, pulling at her miniskirt. Her lips were dark red under the lipstick, now almost completely chewed off; she put them against his, wrinkling her nose, then opened the door to the children whom she gathered about her with the grace of a diva. The blunt cut of their bangs gave them a curious expression of alarm. They were fond of their uncle but seemed to know him less with every visit and now stood sulkily against their mother's long thighs, waiting till they could run to their room.

When he went down, Benoît found his mother busy tidying up the shoes the children had thrown about the hallway. She had put on a tight, rather short dress that was kind to her plumpness, and had mussed up her dyed hair. For all she had made herself look nice, there was no hiding her irritability, which Benoît thought uncalled-for. Seeing him standing at the foot of the stairs, watching Louise soap the children's hands, his mother asked him to go and set the table. They ate in the garden, a simple square of artificial lawn the same width as the house, spreading right up to the living room door and bordered by a fence of old planks with morning glories clinging to it. The view beyond stopped a quarter of a mile away at the edge of the deciduous wood that hid the river, at the far end of an old beetroot field strewn with couch grass and crumpled litter from the road. Louise explained to the children that that was where she used to bury her hamsters when she was little, and Vincent retorted that it was indeed a good place for corpses. His irony made her blush and smile sweetly, and the conversation went no further. The wash hanging between two posts wafted scented shadows across the table. Louise had brought an over-sweet cake, which the journey had wrecked and which was attracting tiny flies in the fine weather. Luc and Fabien did not want any; they both wore the bizarrely contrite expression of scolded little boys. They squirmed in their chairs, harassed by the raw light that glinted on the little clumps of catnip sprouting between the cracks in the empty lot. This house, with its tawdry outlook, aroused in them the fearful disgust of children accustomed to the beauty of newness. Louise rumpled their hair and glanced up at her mother, hoping to raise a smile at their childishness, which she herself looked on favorably. She thought they had gone even blonder, but as no one answered her remark, she began to clear the table. Her mother followed her inside, where she must have questioned her about what was going wrong with Vincent, for Louise was a bit red when she came back. She had brought out the sunscreen and now smeared it over the grimacing faces of the two children. Her intention was to go and sunbathe in the field by the gravel pit; Vincent reacted to the idea as though it offended him and left the table, taking his glass. Louise shot Benoît a smile over Fabien's shoulder. Her indulgence toward Vincent was angelic. She was as gentle as she was slow to rile; she never seemed upset when he got cross with her.

They left at around two. Vincent did not go with them—he claimed he had calls to make and people to see in town—and Benoît was not sorry to escape the condescension their amusements caused him. The children had brought their bikes, which ground over the road in the ruts of dried mud. The gravel pit had been out of use for more than a year now. Yellow broom flower bellied out through the mesh of rusty wire fencing, and a whole section of the leveled area where the trucks used to turn had collapsed among thistles and giant hogweed. A kind of cableway for carrying the gravel over the river formed a supple, fluid line over the perfume-drenched relics. Louise noted the changes without surprise. She had sat down on a rusty girder to re-tie Fabien's laces. Behind her the quarry, like a great white bite out of the hillside, returned the echo of her patient chatter; Benoît threw a stick into it, and it ricocheted lengthily amidst a panic of birds and lizards. The sun-warmed stones gave off a chalky powder that caught in their throats and covered the children in dust. Their hands were chafed from the rubber on the handlebars and they did not understand what they were doing here. Louise blew on their reddened palms and told them she had a hideout way up there near the woods where they could play, and Benoît had to promise to carry the bikes before they would make up their minds to scramble after her along the path by the gravel pit. She walked with astonishing speed in her thick-soled sandals, pulling the children along, one on either side; they made her look like a paper airplane held by its wings.

The area of field at the edge of the void was already half in the shadow of the trees. Louise let go of the children's hands and they stood looking suspiciously at the path they had come along. They always balked at enjoying an outing. Louise stroked the backs of their necks and smiled at Benoît to soothe his impatience with them. The woods gave off a smell of damp moss that made her bare shoulders shake. She seemed to consider a moment before deciding that they would be fine here. The cableway pylon stuck up out of the fields like a stake stabbing into the hill. Fabien whined that it was too high and he was scared, while his brother, seated in the sun on the brow of the gravel pit, took stock of its dizzying height and clamored for cookies. They still could not see what there was to do in this uncomfortable place, but the presence of Benoît, whom they were gradually getting used to again, kept them in suspense.

Louise flattened the grass down with the bath towels and hesitated a moment before getting undressed. Benoît watched her knot her bikini under her T-shirt. She was modest; he remembered having seen her pubic hair only once—at the time, this dark blond tuft had caused him a vague feeling of unease — and later she had let him glimpse the nipples of her swollen breasts when she was pregnant; they were a purplish brown and spread like a splash of oil. They had been strange times, when their daily existence was disrupted by Louise's obstinate happiness. While the two families sought a solution to her refusal to abort, she would spend hours closeted in her brother's room telling him about the transformations that were going on in her. He was then only nine, and he saw Louise as a fallen woman and a sorceress. His mother was irascible, probably believing she could put an end to her daughter's illusions through severity. She had recently separated from her husband, and this marriage seemed even more of a mess to her. Benoît later learned that she had called Louise a fool on the way out of church when she saw her in her doll's dress, hanging on the kiss of a seventeen-year-old husband who had not wanted any part of what he was doing.

They had been there for over an hour. Louise was dozing with her face under an open magazine, the pages humming in the wind. The shadow from the woods had caught up with her, obliging her to pull a white cotton sweater over her bikini. She had not managed to stand up to the children, who had wanted to eat the cookies intended for four o'clock, and the crumpled wrappers rolled down the field to the river. She had listened to them whining that they were bored, sympathetic but also totally powerless to amuse them, then she had shut her eyes, asking them in an innocent voice that was supposed to be commanding

(Benoît thought she did quite a good impression of a real mommy) to keep quiet. Benoît himself was slightly bored, too. Dampness from the ground was soaking through the towels; there was not much pleasure in lying around doing nothing. The sun had slipped into the quarry and from its depths rose the promise of seaside heat. Benoît suggested a skree-run to the children, and they wriggled at the prospect as though it pinched them. Louise raised her head to watch what was going on; Benoît just caught a glimpse of her face squinting in the intense light as they disappeared down the hill.

The children had reached the bottom of the pit and were waiting for Benoît to find them a new game. Their strident voices caused tiny avalanches all around in the silence; their nostrils and arms were powdery with white dust. Right overhead, the imposing loading stage against the pylon cast its jagged shadow across them. Benoît lifted the children one behind the other onto the ladder leading up to it; the extreme narrowness of their hips in their shorts caused him an unexpected wave of emotion. He was starting to enjoy this afternoon. The children crept up the pylon disarmingly slowly. Louise watched from where she was for a few seconds, her smile just visible above the stalks of grass, then, probably thinking them too timid to come to any harm, she pulled her long sweater over her naked thighs and lay down again. Fabien had reached the loading stage and Luc was about to join him, his muscles bracing his girlishly thin body like elastic bands. From here the hollow of the gravel pit looked almost flat and the scent of broom was more marked. Benoît sat down between the two children; they were red to the roots of their hair with the effort, their hands sticky with rust and sweat. Louise lay propped on her elbows and was watching them again between the strands of hair falling over her face. Her response to the danger was childish and delightful; Benoît shouted to her that there was nothing to worry about and she merely nodded in assent.

The shadow from the woods had reached the loading stage and already taken the edge off the kids' enthusiasm, and it was, in a way, to avoid disappointing them that Benoît came up with the idea of sending them down in one of the gondolas along the cable, the way he remembered having seen tons of pebbles glide through the white mist, while the mechanical shovels waved about and ate into the hillside. The children took a moment to understand and get excited. Benoît put them on the platform, and they stood there looking stunned by the empty space. Louise had stood up, too, her long sweater tight under her bottom like a shell. She was uneasy about what they were doing and, when Benoît explained his idea, she frowned in a strange expression of sympathy. She watched her children sit down in the sort of little cart hanging higher up the cable over the loading stage. The wind had picked up and the bath towel flapped against her ankles like a wave. The two children sat facing one another in the gondola and laughed at their own daring. Louise shouted to them to hold on tight to the edge, and there was a note of panic in her voice that Benoît could not hear from where he was.

The cable ran down and disappeared over the tumble of bushes hiding the river, crossing the entire length of the gravel pit a bare six feet above the ground. Benoît swung on it to check the rigidity of this colossus sticking out of the natural world, then began to push the gondola to get it going. But the jaw of little wheels gripping the cable stuck fast and Benoît nearly gave up. The children's excitement was wearing thin while they waited, and they were already looking a bit ruefully down the long, gently sloping drop that plunged into the light. And it was just as they were about to get back out onto the loading stage that Luc noticed a sort of brake clamping the cable where it joined the pylon. Benoît released it and the gondola gently started off with the steady noise of rolling metal. Benoît steered it to the edge of the loading stage. Impatience suddenly flooded the children's faces. They did not take their eyes off their hands, as though to stop them letting go. Benoît let them languish for a moment in the air, while Louise moved a bit closer to get a better look, holding her hair on her shoulder with both hands as though clinging to a rope. She was too nice to stop anyone and just told them again to be careful.

When the gondola at last began to go down, the two children let out a cry of astonishment that was whipped away by thin air. Against all expectations, the contraption almost immediately picked up considerable speed and slid down the cable like a falling stone. Benoît saw the two little wind-blown heads shoot off like missiles. In the few seconds the descent lasted, neither he nor Louise dared stop smiling for fear of invoking a danger they could not in fact imagine. The gondola reached the pylon on the far side of the river at the height of its momentum and flew all but horizontally, tipping Luc and Fabien, who hung like sacks over the side. Louise gave a cry that was cut short by the din of metal on metal as the gondola fell heavily on the children against the pylon. It was as brief as the clash of a cymbal. Already, the gondola had come to a standstill, releasing the children, who slumped into the tall grass.

The cable swayed gently. Louise and Benoît stood rooted to the spot, waiting for the children to emerge from the flowers where they had vanished. She had stopped shouting, perhaps she had even stopped breathing. The almost perfect silence that followed the echo of the impact against the pylon was broken only by the rustle of the fields and the trickle of little pieces of cliff collapsing down the slope. Benoît's head and mind were buzzing so much that he did not immediately hear Louise asking him to go see. Her shrill request suggested no hint of blame, but already the seeds of an irrational hope made her lips tremble slightly. The wall of trees behind her had darkened; she was rubbing her legs together almost imperceptibly and holding her hands flat on her hair to contain the mess the wind was making of it. It was impossible to say whether she was cold or scared, or if she was about to start stamping her feet. So as not to see the spark of demented faith that was sustaining her go out, Benoît clambered down the pylon and ran to the river. His feet sank into the avalanches of gravel slipping from under him. The effort brought a taste of fire to the pit of his lungs. His eyes and mouth were full of tears, but though his body hurt, his mind still felt nothing, as though he had been stunned or stupefied by the enormity of what had just happened.

He grazed his shin on a rock as he crossed the river and his impatience flared with a pain that was akin to pleasure. Louise's eyes followed him like a beggar; Benoît had the feeling he was moving in a dream, driven by her madness. He was now only a short distance from the foot of the pylon and he could already see the hollow the children had made in the flowers. He was so distraught that he felt as though he could no longer see anything and was desperately breathing his own blood. Barely conscious of what he was doing, he parted the grass on one side, then the other, saw the colorful splash of a child's shorts in the grass, and then a face with half-closed lips; the peaceful sight cast a sort of fog over his fears. That they had not been disfigured left room for hope, perhaps the possibility of forgiveness. Benoît did not try to see more; he felt as though he were floating in himself, a long, long way from any real sensation. So he climbed back up the ruins of the old construction site through the jungle of flowers. Louise was coming along the path, hobbling in her unfastened sandals. She appeared to be naked under her long sweater; she had left everything behind, and the bath towels, which the wind had overturned, lay in a heap in the field. Benoît showed her where to cross the river; he would have liked never to have to look at her face.

When she drew level with him, Benoît knew from her

crazed expression that she was already and forever refusing to hear anything anyone said to her. The idea of having to go get help or stay to keep watch when she dared neither to stay here alone nor go without him had absorbed all her capacity for suffering. Benoît promised her that if they walked fast they could be at the house in ten minutes. She was worried about the bikes, then, realizing that it was unimportant, she finally started walking. Benoît glanced furtively at her. Her cheeks were very red and she had her hand over her mouth, probably so as not to scream or vomit. She seemed curiously reckless to him, and at the same time completely impervious to the catastrophe. And, at that moment, the impression that the children had felt nothing and that Louise was incapable of imagining the drama that had just occurred distanced him from the catastrophe. Louise wanted to run a bit but stopped almost immediately, writhing with a sudden sharp pain in her side. Her nostrils flared broadly; probably she too had the feeling she was breathing blood. Benoît wondered if she realized that both her children were dead.

II

No one had cried out. Of the hours that followed, Benoît retained the memory of a staggering bewilderment while everyone tried to keep from falling, as though this might still prevent something. Louise refused to go back there. She had had an incomprehensible burst of hysterics when she realized that she had come home without her skirt, then something in her had suddenly given way, she had to be carried to her room and Benoît had left on his own with Vincent in the ambulance. He had told them which road to take and said straight out that the children must be dead in an instinctive and almost unconscious move to dump on to others a tragedy that was far beyond his strength. It was a beautiful day, the sun folded them in pleasant, spring warmth that smelled of molten plastic seating. The ambulance crew showed them a sort of mute respect, which Vincent seemed to distrust. He was sniffling and mumbling insults, his tears exploding in fat bubbles on his lips. Benoît avoided meeting his gaze in the rearview mirror. Fear of the reactions he would have to endure was numbing his mind. He had the feeling that he was tumbling unbelievably slowly, as though into a hole, toward the certainty of disaster. Yet the memory of the little face intact among the flowers harbored a sweet gentleness that was entirely at odds with the gravity of what they were experiencing. In truth, he could not believe how simply one could topple into a nightmare.

The gravel pit's white arena was now in shadow. Higher up, the bath towels lay in a heap in the grass, the pages of the magazine still fluttering in the wind. It already seemed a long time ago. Benoît could hear the blood pounding in his ears. He pointed to the spot where the children had fallen and remained standing by the car crying, overwhelmed by a growing sense of pity. The two ambulance men took stock of the terrain before heading down the steep slope with its cover of bushes. Vincent followed a short distance behind, parting the grass with his tall, still adolescent body like a swimmer. The two men had now reached the pylon; they asked Vincent to go back to the river, then stood a long time bending over the flowers as though looking down a well—Benoît suddenly felt sure the children were no longer there and that none of this could have happened. Vincent shifted from one foot to the other in the vast shelter of the gaping cliff, and shot him a smile of exaggerated confidence. Everything was happening in the utmost calm, as though they had in half an hour acquired an extremely adult knowledge of the worst. Benoît followed the moves of the party through the glitter of the tears blurring his eyes. Already the two men were lifting the bodies; they were frozen into a twisted position that gave him a shock: death was now neither miraculous nor improbable. Benoît saw himself once again helping the children into the gondola, and this vision suddenly took on its monstrous meaning, although he could not reconcile himself to it. The men had stuffed the bodies into white bags and carried them to the ambulance in their arms. Vincent spat several times between his feet. He glared at the two men with an expression of baffled hatred. Benoît told himself that it all had to stop; it seemed incredible that this was now reality.

The sun had completely disappeared off the side of the hill. In the green depths of the gorge the river rolled its pebbles along with the rumble of billiard balls; Vincent and Benoît felt chilly and out of place in this corner of nature redolent with the smells of evening, but there were still the beach things to fetch and the bikes already frosted with damp. Benoît saw one of the men carefully folding the towels, the magazine, and Louise's miniskirt and Vincent tugging at the bikes to disentangle the pedals. Their gestures seemed somehow absurd and necessary. And Benoît suddenly felt nothing but the acute sensation of his own existence.

When they got back, Vincent fell by degrees into a delirium of revenge. The crisis had closed over them for good this time, leaving not even room to breathe. Quite simply because there was no other truth possible, Benoît explained that the children had climbed into the gondola without him knowing and the brake had immediately released. Vincent listened with a crazed half-smile to this version of blamelessness that was an insult to his pain. He had turned in his seat to stare at Benoît and somehow identify the source of the blows that were torturing him so much. His look was almost threatening. The kindness of the ambulance crew, as they tried to keep him in check, antagonized him; again and again he pushed them off the way he would have defended himself with a stick. The whole thing made Benoît feel so sick and afraid that he could not even cry; he said he wanted to throw up, asked to be dropped off at the house, and sat as though deaf with his forehead against the window, waiting in a state of emergency and eternity for the nightmare to end or retreat.

It was past six o'clock but the sun was still high behind the trees with their fresh leaves. As they turned off the road that led to the pit, Benoît caught sight of the tackle belonging to a group of fishermen who were coming back up from the river, and the injustice of his lot, reduced to nothing in a second, sucked him over a new precipice. Vincent had stiffened as they approached the house, now visible ahead on the main road among the gray-brown relief of fields. Benoît sat motionless, so overcome with fear that it no longer seemed to affect his consciousness. The shutters to Louise's bedroom were closed and his mother was waiting in the doorway. As they pulled into the parking area, Benoît realized that she was still dressed for receiving visitors; but he saw, too, that she had put on a pair of flat, down-at-heel shoes and that the makeup was gone from her face. From her brief glance toward the back of the van, Benoît understood that she had been told the worst straight away. She moved sharply toward the door, as though to wrest her son from the contagion of death, then just aimed a word of thanks in the direction of the two men as the ambulance drove off. Vincent turned to them with his fist raised threateningly, but his face in the background showed his sudden terror as he drove off to the morgue.

When Vincent came home in the early evening, his violence had taken a disturbingly crazed form. It was starting to grow cool and they could only just make out the distant shape of the woods in the gathering dusk. Benoît was waiting in the living room; he had turned out all the lights so as not to see himself in the windowpanes. Inaction was endlessly exacerbating his torment. Louise had not left her room for three hours, and there had been from it no moan or cry which would nevertheless have been far preferable to this silence. Her mother waited at the top of the steps for Vincent to appear; she was dreading his reaction and rushed into the hall to bar his way upstairs. Yet Vincent did not seem to realize what she was doing there, facing him. He was feverish, as though his body itched. He seemed to find his misery so intolerable that he had to cause pain in his turn. Under the electric light in the hallway his nervousness appeared inordinate. Benoît would have liked him to go away. The inevitability of their plight gripped him like a fist; he could think of nothing other than this fear that was anesthetizing him.

Vincent sank into an armchair after haunting the corridor for a long time. His pain and hatred found no expression and seemed to harass him terribly. Benoît felt awed by his agony; he could see that Vincent had the children's death before his eyes and that the image was appalling and, most curiously, that it was one which he and Louise had somehow been spared.

Benoît took over from his mother minding Louise once people began to arrive. Vincent's parents came later that evening. They had traveled without stopping, and the smell of the overheated hood lingered for several seconds under the still open windows. Benoît saw the squat shadow of the father disappear into the house, then heard him shouting that he wanted to have a word with Louise. His voice reached them through the floor in short, strident bursts that made her roll in her bed like a lump of wood. She covered her ears and looked at Benoît with the same smile of impossible hope she had had when she had told him to run down to the pylon. The image of the two little heads sailing through the whiteness of the quarry and of the bodies falling soundlessly into the flowers cast a sort of spell over the tragedy. Benoît could not have said if Louise was conscious, nor if he himself felt anything other than a sense of the unreal. The evening smelled of spring and, now and again, of fuel from the road. A cat prowled mewing around the pile of scrap metal in the faint glimmer from the windows. Louise lay huddled on the bed; she was starting to run a temperature. She still wore her long white sweater and had pulled on a pair of pajama bottoms that were baggy at the knees. Her mouth was a painful, blood red and her cheeks were flushed. Benoît would have liked to talk to her but was far too afraid of the things they might say to each other. Staying seated was becoming more and more uncomfortable; the hubbub from downstairs was fusing with the noise in his mind. Louise's sleep-like torpor oppressed him perhaps more than his fear of confronting the others. So he leaned his elbows on the windowsill and watched his tears floating in the darkness. He would barely have guessed that the woods were there, in the distance; at the corner of the house the light from the living room spilled out onto the gravel of the parking lot, where a big, torn cardboard box was flapping in the darkness. Who was still down there, and what could they have to tell each other on a night like this? Benoît had no more tears, just this distress clutching at his throat. He tried to concentrate on the absence of the children, but his obsessions returned continually to the present moment.

Around one o'clock, Benoît was alerted by a sudden noise of footsteps and doors opening and closing, and almost immediately his mother came into the room with a doctor. She had powdered her face to hide its redness; under their swollen lids her eyes had the intensity of the days when she was late coming home. Seeing her children caught up in a tragedy like this made her a moving figure of grief and rage. She repeated several times, as she clasped

Benoît's arm, that there was nobody left downstairs and that Vincent and his parents had gone to sleep with friends in town. She clung to anything that might seem to offer comfort, and this departure did. Louise was shading her eyes from the overhead light, submitting to the doctor's compassion with the docility of a defeated lover. Her face was shiny with fever and expressed irrational gratitude. Her mother dabbed at her eyes and kept smiling at her. Benoît had never known her to be so emotional about them; this first night of grieving left him long afterward with the memory of an extraordinary depth of feeling.

Louise's temperature did not go down for several days, not while the questions lasted. Without even knowing, she had given the same version of the accident as Benoît, depriving herself forever, and although she would have wanted it, of all hope of absolution. Their mother made no attempt to know any more, instinctively dismissing even a hint of a disaster that was quite inconceivable. With every visit, she minded their answers as though minding a treasure that needed protecting. She could have spent hours protesting nonstop that they were in no way to blame for the whole thing.

Louise became hysterical as they were about to leave for the funeral, and Benoît stayed home with her on the instructions of their mother, who was trying to preserve in him an element of carefree innocence, however tenuous, for later on when they would once more have to think about living and—why not—being happy. It was hot in the house and over the fields, where the emerald shimmer of corn was just emerging from the earth. Louise lay across the covers, her eyes wide open, her smooth belly hardly rising in the gap in her pajamas. Benoît watched over the strange peace of her grief, his love for her intensified by his total inability to show it. And it was during these two, motionless hours, while he silently reproached himself for leaving her comfortless, that he learned, at Louise's expense, to force himself above all not to think.

They lived for a few more days in the turbulence of visits. Vincent's anger had finally changed into an aggressive taciturnity that was painful to witness. The evening after the funeral he came home drunk and was so sick that it finally put him on a par with the general mourning. His attacks against Louise and Benoît were exhausted, his agony seemed suddenly unfocused. He went back to sleeping with Louise and spent the afternoons at the house answering letters, sometimes sitting for hours at a time with his eyes glued to the open pages of the phone book. His parents came only at rare intervals, as if the house were abhorrent to them, or as if they wanted to protect the family from themselves and from the need for justice that must remain eternally frustrated. Benoît preferred it this way: above all, seeing and knowing nothing of their grief.

Benoît went back to school the following Monday and his mother returned to work, as though they were settling into their transfigured life for good. It was grayer, cooler. A fine, fog-like rain shrouded the wasteland. Louise was emerging from her lethargy. Her face was slightly hollow and her body thinner still. She began to get dressed again and come to the table to eat. Her parents-in-law came to keep her company on the mornings when her mother was at work. They were trying to make peace with the place, and this effort gave them a fussy awkwardness with her. Her sleepwalker's grief and beachwear disconcerted them, the way her manner of running her household disconcerted them. She was too lovable for them to resent her, but her behavior remained an exasperating mystery to them. So they struggled with their anger, unable to face blaming her for such a hideous death, and simply suffered all the more as a result. There was soon talk of them going back down south and Louise joining them. For a long time she rejected the idea, which seemed to burn her and which Vincent endorsed only half-heartedly. One morning, however, she resigned herself to it, on a noiseless Sunday with no traffic, when the sky had stood still for days, filling her with an almost tangible dismay, which she had probably hoped to escape for a time by giving in. Benoît hardly dared admit that he was relieved to see her despair move farther off. Her mother did nothing to hold her back, either; nevertheless, this resignation soon turned out to be powerless to bring her the slightest comfort.

They left at around midday. The two cars were to follow one behind the other for five hours under a cloudless sky that held the world in a hothouse heat. Louise had spent the morning looking at but not reading the numerous letters she had received. She was wearing dark glasses and her mouth below was like an open wound of tears and life. Vincent sat and smoked on the car hood, keeping an eye on the road his parents were to come along. Their couple had lost its meaning; Benoît wondered what alleged habit or superstition made everyone determined to see them together. He was already sorry for his cowardliness toward Louise, but there again, he did not know how to show this or tell her about it.

His mother had not had the strength to watch the car drive off. Benoît found her bending over a basket of washing in the bathroom. She asked him to help her fold the sheets, and for an instant he told himself that nothing had changed. They ate the remains of the previous day's dinner in front of the television. Benoît realized the untold effort she was making to keep from howling with pain. Yet they did not open up to one another, did not touch one another, and thus acquired the habit of suppressing all emotion, because both refused, with the energy of ogres, pleasure-seekers, or bandits, to let the misfortune overwhelm them more than it had done already.

Benoît wanted to go and join his friends, but he felt it was inappropriate.

The sun and wind returned the day after Louise's departure. All morning the house lay wide open to the thunder of cars. Benoît had a sense of appalling emptiness. There were fewer visits and phone calls. Through negligence or ill temper his mother had shunned the friendships that were forthcoming at the time of her divorce; she had got on relatively well with the solitude she lived in and did nothing to encourage anyone's sympathy. Already the painful magic of the first days was ceasing to operate. They were starting to get bored and irritated again; sometimes they even thought about other things. Even the images of the accident, the field's implacable stillness after the fall and Louise's face frozen hysterically as she stumbled along the path, no longer seemed so real. Benoît was getting used to living with this terror, which seemed as though it, too, might fade, especially because the cruelty of the rumors that went around for a time about the circumstances of the accident had hardened him in his version of the truth and militated against blame in spite of himself. He felt, finally, increasingly forsaken, though this had nothing to do with the children's death, which his heart could not take in, and he woke every morning to the violent shock of the memory of Louise lying inert and stricken across the bed. From time to time he saw his friends again. They were intimidated by this bereavement, and as they loafed about wordlessly in the now green woods of the neighborhood, his revolt grew. His mother kept an eye on him; he could feel her ready to shout out when he came in nervously from school or when she saw him hanging listlessly about the rooms. Her own pain was directly informed and fed by Louise and Benoît's—probably she had finally conceived an impious and healthy rage about the children's death, for he never heard her mention their memory.

The bereavement imposed on them a still greater lack of privacy that was becoming irksome. His mother had got a bit plumper and seemed to be stifling in her dresses. She smelled different and she now did her face every day to hide her fatigue. Benoît dodged her attempts at comfort—the way she had of dismissing his dejection with a brisk wave of her hand. He guessed that she was waiting for a call and that this new torment was worrying her far more than her qualms about thinking of her love life in these circumstances. He knew next to nothing about this very spasmodic relationship, already several years old, and he had avoided happening onto anything to do with it. The fact was, he had never liked hearing her getting ready or seeing her happy in this way. His own knowledge of pleasure, experienced with timorous girls with tight, tepid vaginas, put him off the idea of his mother's encounters. She hid her anxiety pretty well, but stayed up later and later and cried more bitterly. Every evening, she would jump when the phone rang, and her disappointment when she failed to recognize the man she was expecting doubtless added cruelly to the pain of hearing her daughter's voice growing continually fainter. Louise never had much to tell them; she complained of nothing, she was inaccessible. Benoît could tell just from his mother's voice, harsh with fear and bitterness, the point at which Louise's attention was wandering, like a broken mooring. Hearing her so distant and hurt like this soon became intolerable. And before long, it became obvious to all of them that she should come back and live with them. This time, the parents-in-law did not protest. They explained that everyone's grief was different and that their efforts to help one another had turned into a fraught and exhausting game, but the pain was still unbearable. They were worn out by the daily scenes of tears. Louise did not understand the exasperation she aroused and her in-laws could not forgive themselves for causing her further pain. Seeing her leave brought them a relief which, they claimed, conflicted for a few days with the guilt of sending her away.

Louise came back two days later, six weeks to the day after the children's funeral. Benoît placed great hope in this return, as though Louise was going to come back miraculously cured. He spent the day tidying up the garage in the bracing nausea of oil warmed by the summer that was flourishing outside. For her part, Louise got her things ready and sorted out photos of the children; in the evening on the phone her voice already seemed closer to them. Benoît promised he would paint her room and come and meet her at the crossroads. Talking and, he thought, being happy together was getting easier. Benoît was touched: he felt as though he had no right to go out after their conversation and had gone to listen to music on his bed.

A thick fog rose off the fields and slowed the nightly convoy of eighteen-wheelers. The string of pale lamps and the hum of engines pleasantly wearied his mind so that he did not immediately hear his mother knocking. He wanted to open the door but she stopped him from turning the handle with surprising strength. They wrestled like this for a fraction of a second and Benoît's suspicions were aroused. She was expecting someone and did not want him to go down. He could smell her perfume through the door and was choked by the thought that she was already made up to go out. As she got no answer, she knocked on the door again and asked if he had heard. He gave a louder thump in reply and threw himself on his bed. He hated her.

Nearly an hour later, light shone on the front of the house. Benoît turned the music down. A car door banged, then came the measured tread of someone calmly checking out the grounds. His mother's "Good evening" rose very distinctly in the half-light. Her voice was cheerful, or simply changed. Benoît did not even glance out of the window. For what seemed an eternity, he heard the television jabbering away in the living room and his mother giving bursts of sudden, sad laughter. Then she came upstairs to tell him she was going out. Again, there was the noise of measured footsteps on the driveway, and the garage door lit up with two big yellow halos, which cut through the fog and slowly sank into the seething drizzle. Benoît went downstairs, kicking the banisters as he went. Darkness on the ground floor was not quite total and he looked in vain for signs of the man who had been there. The silence was still sugary with his mother's perfume. Outside, night was starting to fall, but when he put the light on, the reflection of the room in the window panes looked even more cheerless. It was too late to call Louise or go and knock at a friend's house. Benoît felt a sense of injustice and jealousy. He buried his face in the sofa cushions and sobbed for the first time in weeks.

He was woken at about two in the morning by the rattle of a key in the lock and just had time to dash into his room. His mother did not put the light on; she stayed quietly in the dark for nearly a quarter of an hour. Benoît heard her put her shoes under the stairs, walk barefoot and a bit breathless upstairs, and lock herself in her room. Then he heard a smothered wail like a groan from the ends of the earth. Whom or what was she crying about? It made Benoît feel better to think she was suffering. He crept out of his room to go and listen on the landing, but at the first creak of the floorboards his mother ordered him back to bed. Her voice through the door sounded more angry than distraught, which piqued his curiosity. Even hating her was beginning to depress him. He tried to concentrate on the joy of Louise coming home and finally fell asleep.

The fog dispersed with the day, gradually unveiling a shifting, early summer sky. At about midday, a dazzling flash of lightning lit the empty lot where a brief shower was stirring up the dry dirt, and Benoît decided to relieve his impatience by cycling to the crossroads. The car appeared around the bend the moment he came to the stop sign, and his heart began to pound so wildly, as he caught sight of Louise's motionless face behind the windscreen, that he had to put his foot to the ground. The big chest of drawers strapped to the car roof gave a lurch as Vincent hurtled past him, honking. Louise had wound down the window to shout something to him that was lost in the wake of the car. She kept her head out of the window and watched the distance open up between them, like a gulf separating them already. There was something heartbreaking about her troubled smile within the hair tumbling about her face; Benoît had to stop again to calm his agitation.

Louise had put back on the few pounds she had lost during her fever; she was wearing a very short, white backless top and a brick-red skirt, also short. Her skin was golden with blond down, and her lips had that juicy, plum-swollen translucence that made her beauty so incredibly powerful. It was amazing how the life in her struggled against calamity, and how moving this made calamity. Benoît had gone to put his bike away and his mother must have been drying her eyes somewhere in the house, so that Louise, who had brought a dessert and CDs for her brother, seemed suddenly embarrassed by her gifts as though by an inappropriate confession. She smiled but did not kiss them so as not to spoil the moment with tears, too sweet-natured to upset anyone with her grief. The sun was already hot and was drying up the rain, spreading mist over the tarmac with the pleasing smell of laundry; it was one of those poignant moments life derisively held in store for them. Behind them, Vincent was looking at the landscape while scratching the back of his neck; he thought he too would settle here; Benoît wondered why no one had even thought of it.

The couple's worldly goods consisted of four cases, two of them full of the children's things, and a stout chest of drawers lashed to the car roof and filled with CDs and shoes. Benoît helped Vincent take it upstairs. They sweated with the effort in the post-shower humidity. Vincent had rolled up his shirt sleeves and the veins and muscles stood out in his bony arms. He had the colossal strength of a man on the run, a survivor, and indeed, this move was an escape: he had not followed Louise, he had run away from his parents. His attitude toward Benoît was more brotherly; they must have spotted some similarity in one another, something in common. It was during the quarter hour they spent shifting furniture, in the smell of old wood and perspiration, that their odd friendship took root, or, rather, their tacit brotherhood in burglary.

They had lunch in the garden. Vincent sat and ate, head down in silence, like a miscreant caught red-handed and waiting for a moment to get away. In spite of the fine weather, Louise had put on a thick, white cotton sweater that seemed to be making her sleepy; her face in its smooth frame of hair was oddly imperturbable. Neither his mother nor Benoît dared look at her, and their unease made them screw up their eyes from time to time. She must have felt at fault for the silence and discomfort they were in, for throughout the meal she forced herself to smile through the constant depression that was stifling her, interminably chewing food which her body refused to swallow. In the resounding health of her slim body and silky cheeks, her soul was drowning. Such want of strength made her courage all the more touching. Benoît watched her out of the corner of his eye, sick for her and unhappy that he had neither the heart nor the courage to cope with her like this. Probably neither did his mother, still less Vincent. They were too strong for her, as she must already have realized. It was a bit as though she had come to lose herself here since she could not survive anywhere else.

At about two, Louise went upstairs to lie down, and the whole family felt relieved. Benoît wondered what they would do during this shattered eternity that yawned before them, stunning them. Vincent's lips were stained with the wine he had brought. He offered Benoît a cigarette, looking, with an oddly aggressive air, now at the cracked ground of the empty lot, now at his mother-in-law who was clearing the table. When she had gone to wash the dishes, he put his elbows on the table and sat staring at Benoît, about to say something apparently crucial but impossible to articulate. He was probably the most affected of them because he was the least good at being charitable. Benoît had never really liked him but he was not averse to the idea of having an older companion permanently around, someone smarter on whom marriage imposed no obvious timetable. It had cleared up completely now; a hazy savannah light shimmered over the surrounding fields. Upstairs, the curtains at Louise's bedroom window swayed gently, inducing a sleep that was most likely dreamless. Vincent told them she took tranquilizers and sometimes slept for whole days. Benoît sensed Vincent was more annoyed than sorry about all this, having to grope about in a new life where he did not know the rules and could find no way out, and which would certainly never again be peaceful for him. Benoît felt a mix of fear and reticence. Vincent had never been particularly nice to Louise and would probably be less and less so. He was a surly character with a destructive streak, and the children's death, or more likely doubts and anger, had made him even harsher.

When he had finished his wine, Vincent suggested going for a drive, and, given all the dead time of the previous month, the prospect seemed a happy one. They shared, at least, the same impatience and felt the same need to blot out thought; this chance companionship would do for a time. Benoît went to tell his mother that they were going out. She must have been crying, for her eyes were even more startlingly blue; she reacted with an unexpected "good riddance" aimed at her son-in-law. Benoît could not get over how one could persist in disliking someone in these circumstances. Her bad faith had the effect of reconciling him to Vincent's relative arrogance.

It was a Saturday at the beginning of June, one of those dishearteningly splendid days with too much light. Vincent bypassed S. and headed for the motorway. He seemed to be toying with the temptation of running away for good and feeling therefore increasingly frustrated. Heat from the windscreen contrasted pleasantly with the fierce wind that whipped their faces through the open windows. Vincent drove fast; Benoît did not much like the expression of his rather deep-set eyes nor the white in his knuckles showing through his skin as he gripped the steering wheel, yet it was the first time since the accident that he felt a bit excited and for this he was grateful. His pals were still hampered by the consideration they thought they owed him. Their meetings had become a sort of awkward obligation, and he went away depressed and lonely. Sometimes he would have preferred the punishment of genuine remorse. He and Vincent were now on the same side, miserable with anger and jealous of other people's luck. Nevertheless, over the couple of hours they spent together amid the thrill of speed and music, Benoît's pleasure continually alternated with the fear that Vincent would finally bring up the question he had been mulling over since lunchtime. The memory of the moment when he had released the brake on the gondola flashed through his mind. It was as though the whole thing suddenly really existed, as though he was coming round to the hard facts after a long spell of amnesia. He had blushed and had lost the feeling in his limbs. Vincent shot him an impassive glance and turned off at the first picnic area. A few cars stood dotted among the pattern of grassy patches, and the empty sky, almost artificially blue, hung above them oppressively. The scent of wild roses floated in the air like the lament of a Portuguese fado. Vincent took out a cigarette and detached the filter with obsessive precision. He had opened his door and was scuffing the grass with his shoe. "Anyway, there's no going back," he said finally, carefully tapping out the ash between his feet. "Don't let anyone tell you what you should be feeling. I mean, no one can imagine what you saw." He was in pain, but his expression was disagreeable. Benoît wondered what he meant. He realized that he hardly knew him and that he was not sure he wanted to like him. The abrupt wave of guilt he felt and the growing disappointment of these get-togethers caused him a kind of moral nausea.

When they got back, Louise was listening to the radio in front of the house, whose shadow was stealing over the empty lot among the poppies growing misshapenly out of the bumps now as hard as concrete. She asked them with a childishly greedy smile if they had had fun. She was hiding her hands in the sleeves of the outsize sweater she had worn before in the gravel pit and which came down to the top of her thighs. Her face was disconcertingly sweet; Benoît felt a pang of love for her, and the feeling cleansed him of the mix of fascination, excitement, and guilt left over from his excursion with Vincent. He told her where they had been. Louise was looking him in the eyes but had already stopped listening. Benoît again had the impression that she was drowning in herself and that her words were bubbles rising miraculously up to them. He would have kissed her but for the gut fear he felt that she would start to cry.

On Monday, Vincent began to look for work and Benoît was not sorry to be, as it were, relieved of the temptations of his friendship. There were still a few weeks to go before the holidays, but his teachers accepted his absences out of respect for the bereavement, an indulgence he sometimes felt he had no right to, because his grief was of so different a nature. The weather continued fine and it was starting to be hot. Louise had taken down the curtains at her window as though undoing the buttons on a collar that was too tight, and in the morning they could hear the noise of birds and traffic through the door of her room. Benoît often went in to keep her company. Mostly, he found her sitting by the window, an open magazine on her lap. She would look up at him with a disarming start, her dark glasses forming two holes in her face, and Benoît was in agony for her. It was as though it choked her to smile. Her movements seemed to have become even slower, her strained face was now as gracious and majestic as a Madonna's. Her mother anxiously took note of these transformations, of her astonishing calm and her uneasy chats with her brother. Seeing them both awkward and broken sometimes brought out a brutal energy in her. They never heard her cry. She did the cooking every day, went back to wearing the mildly sexy dresses of a still-pretty woman, and showed them a rough, unaccustomed tenderness which Benoît, with his seventeen-year-old virility, often found embarrassing. He had been seeing Elodie, an old school friend, again for a while and was constantly aroused by the gravity of her pitying face, the sour-sweet smell of her hair, and her childishly slim body, and his mother's rough teasing sat unpleasantly on his desire.

Elodie was supposed to come and wait for him that evening after supper, but Vincent was late getting home, causing a general feeling of irritation to hover over the meal, and Benoît dared not slip away. Behind the dark outline of the woods, daylight lingered on, endlessly mocking his hesitation. Vincent had wanted to watch a war film, whose convoluted plot mesmerized them. Benoît resented them for keeping him here. Vincent had been hot in the car, and his smell, together with that of his mother, who, he guessed, was again hoping for (or worrying about) a call, made him uncomfortable. Even Louise's gentleness as she dozed against Vincent's arm was getting him down.

He went up to his room at about eleven. Vincent and Louise were already in bed; after a while, he heard them arguing on the other side of the wall, their voices rising and falling in a kind of rumble. Benoît suddenly realized that he would be able to hear them making love and his spirits fell at the thought. Outside, the stillness of the night was almost tomb-like, broken now and again by the lights of a car as it plunged into the illuminated roads beyond. Benoît had not made his bed; the sheets were still warm from the afternoon sun and felt limp against his skin. It was too heavy to sleep, so he changed his T-shirt and went downstairs. His mother was waiting by the phone in the living room, probably without hope and in vain. She had done her hair again and did not notice him going out. He had hardly closed the door when he heard his name in the dark. Elodie was half hidden in a corner of the garage; the crunch of his soles rang far into the night. She seemed as anxious about approaching as she was about not being seen. Benoît told her she was stupid to have waited so long; in fact, he was thrilled to pieces.

She was wearing a stretch cotton dress and was getting cold. Benoît led her behind the house but never managed to persuade her to cross the partial darkness of the empty lot where the roadside billboards cast their gigantic shadows. They stayed propped against the gable, exposed like deserters to the sudden intrusion of headlights sweeping across the fields from half a mile away. Elodie clung to his hand, her eyes shining in the pale neon light that strayed over the uneven ground. Benoît kissed her but her mouth did not really respond to his. She was nervous about being there and probably uncomfortable. He managed to raise her skirt but did not get beyond the warm folds of her panties clenched between her legs. So, unable to stand it any longer, he undid his belt and under her gaze, unzipped completely. She glanced briefly toward the road then held her hair back and began to clasp his penis with an almost comical vigor. It was not very pleasant being stroked like this, but Benoît was so aroused that he came in a few minutes. She drew back smartly to avoid being soiled, then took a few cautious steps along the wall, looking for somewhere to wipe her hand among the roots and nettles.

When this strange exercise was over, they could find almost nothing to say to one another and now dared not even touch. In an adult voice that was at variance with the clumsiness of her ministrations, Elodie told him she was going away for the weekend with her parents and that she would call. No more cars had passed for a time; the silence gave out all sorts of vague rustles. Accustomed to the dark, their eyes suddenly made out a truck that had stopped at the far edge of the cornfield. Elodie was scared and wanted to leave immediately. Benoît kissed her again, this time more successfully, more slow and moist, then he walked her to the road from where he watched her run off, turning now and again and discreetly sniffing her hand. When her figure finally reappeared in the distance, in the light from the street lamps, he went to drink from the garage tap then went indoors. His mother had gone up to bed without switching the light out behind her; the sofa still held her shape and perfume. The house was totally silent, as though it had held its breath so as not to disturb him. Benoît was on edge. Desire still nagged at his prick like an itch till he thought he would never be able to pee. His mouth, rubbed up and swollen by their kisses, smiled back at him from the mirror. He thought back to how Louise used to come home from her first dates with Vincent and would violently pull at her lips to keep up that wounded beauty which she thought feminine, and he wondered why such a thing had happened to this couple who were so beautiful.

He was woken at about eight o'clock by a window slamming to in a sudden gust of wind. A sort of minor storm was stirring up the gravel on the parking lot. Beyond the fields, a thick, dirty yellow sky had gathered over the tops of the buildings. Benoît was bothered by the feel of Elodie's fingers on his prick and by a vague sense of remorse, which he dismissed. He pulled on a cotton sweater and felt its roughness pleasant against his skin. The sounds of water and people walking about downstairs filled him with misgivings that were confirmed as soon as he went down. Louise was wiping the kitchen table with the slowness of an idiot; her eyes had vanished under their puffy lids and her sorrow had taken another, more anxious form. Could there be new suffering, worse than having seen her children die? Benoît stood dumbfounded before this grief-stricken face, unbearable in its despair. Pity swept through him with the heat of alcohol, but he could find nothing to say. His mother motioned to him to leave his sister alone. She, too, wore an expression of utter dejection and a smile that verged on tears, which presumably explained why she was letting herself be late for work. Vincent had his back to them, seated in the wind outside the French door to the garden, both hands clasped behind his head. Benoît dared not ask what was going on; in any case, it was unlikely anyone would reply. He thought back to the muffled argument he had heard the previous evening, and he was cross with all of them for not being more sensible.

Louise drifted into the living room like a ghost and went to join Vincent on the steps. She sat down timidly a couple of feet away from him and, for what seemed rather a long moment, they both stared in silence at the bleak mess of the empty lot. The wind buffeted a crate about but still it did not rain. A wire dangling from the shutter scraped against the pane of glass in the door. Louise looked down at her hands between her knees; her hair was in her mouth. Vincent handed her his cigarette and she dragged on it closing her eyes. She sat still for a long time before breathing out the smoke. Then the cigarette slipped from her fingers, and fat tears appeared under her lowered lashes. And so, when he had crushed the cigarette she had dropped in the grass, Vincent took her by the shoulders and drew her toward him. Such displays of gentleness were rare for him. Benoît was glad he was able to like him a bit. He had never imagined that Louise could still suffer because of this man whom everyone thought she had married without thinking.

Benoît went to make himself a coffee. As he passed the bathroom door, his eyes met his mother's in the mirror; her face was full of bitterness and a terrible look of surprise flashed across it just as she slammed the door. Benoît shouted that he was sick of all this and retreated to the kitchen. An electric ring had been left on and was heating the gloom. Benoît bit into a piece of baguette; it tasted like dust. Outside, Vincent and Louise were disappearing hand in hand into the fog, which was absorbing the threat of a storm and the edges of the woods. When she came back into the kitchen, his mother shot the pair of them an unpleasant glance. She was very late but took the trouble before she left to give Benoît a rough, affectionate hug to cheer him up. Her eyes were glittering, dilated with emotion, and her makeup was a bit smudged. "I'm sorry," she muttered finally, as she put her raincoat on. "Your sister is still a child, she doesn't know how to deal with him." Benoît asked what had happened, but she flapped her hand in a funny way to show that it didn't matter although it was so serious. Her breath was a bit stale with nerves and the smell floated in the kitchen long after she had gone.

It was already Friday; Benoît decided not to go to school. He made himself a sandwich and ate it on the steps. The fog had gotten even thicker, and the hiss of rain soon rose from it like a gathering murmur creeping invisibly over the fields and bringing the couple running back. Vincent helped Louise climb over the fence. Her face was radiant and gave her swollen eyes a sort of splendor. Vincent also looked surprisingly pleased with their reconciliation.

They spent the whole morning talking things over, clinging to each other like survivors in the cool dampness of the storm, which stopped the world at the garden fence. Idleness was part of the strange, dangerous pleasures of bereavement. Benoît was faintly concerned about what would become of them, but he comforted himself with the thought that the holidays would soon grant him a break. He was, in fact, still hopeful that things would work out.

That day, Vincent took them out to lunch at an inn a few miles away, above a deep arm of the river. Pattering rain echoed in the semi-deserted room and trickled down the huge bay window, from where, through a gap in the trees, they could see the dirty brown water bubbling along with its debris of leaves and bits of wood. Louise was cold; her arm was misting up the window. She sat huddled under Vincent's arm and ate scarcely anything, a magical expression of admiration and trust on her face still raddled by lack of sleep. He, too, appeared calmer for feeling her so close by. Benoît had never seen him so chatty. When they came to pay, Vincent claimed that he had stolen regularly from his parents since he was twelve. Louise blushed up to the roots of her hair, suddenly seeming to fill with new life, and signaled to her brother not to say anything about, he supposed, the bills she used to bring him in the past. Benoît was amazed she still had such secrets from Vincent after so many years. He described how, when they were little, their mother used to fill their pockets with beauty products before going through the check-out. Louise gazed at him with the eyes of a lover. Her lips looked blue in the neon lighting, Vincent's hand huge on her chilly shoulder.

They came home late in the afternoon. Their mother had been there for an hour; she had been getting worried, but when she heard Louise laugh, her annoyance almost subsided. Rain kept them in till evening. Louise had switched on a little electric fire to dispel the dampness in the room, and staring at its ruddy glow in the half-light she soon dozed off. Over dinner she again seemed in danger of sinking away from them, but Vincent had not let go of her hand, and this little miracle was enough to brighten the evening. Benoît thought about going over to Elodie's, but chose not to risk finding that she was out on a day like this. He went up to his room, put some music on, and pressed his face to the window to stare through the rain at the white foam the trucks were dragging along the road. There was no more light downstairs. In the next room, Louise was making high-pitched murmurs heavy with sobs, but Vincent quite soon managed to soothe her. For the first time in now nearly a month since Louise's return, there was, if not life, at least a modicum of peace in the house.

June ended with storms. The empty lot became a muddy mirror that reflected the whiteness of the sky between each cloudburst. Benoît got up late; the pleasure of the holidays was marred by the boredom of being stuck at home and the excruciating anxiety of living so close to Louise. Twice he had seen Elodie. She received him on her inappropriate child's bed in the intimidating intimacy of huge blue curtains, but already she seemed more reticent. Benoît was an impatient lover. Elodie was slow to pleasure; her numb kisses and prudery put him off. He was cross with her for several days for not coming to see him before going to her grandparents'.

Vincent had just found a job for July and August in a bike shop, and he came home for dinner a bit irritable or sarcastic at knowing they were on holiday and hanging around the house all day. The unusual tenderness between Louise and him had vanished with the clouds, after a week spent huddling together under the same umbrella or on café seats in S. Vincent had been quick to go back to his usual gruffness, and low-voiced arguments erupted again in the heat of the first July evenings, though they now no longer left Louise so distraught. Summer, pink-tinged and orange, paralyzed the area in lethargy and silence. Louise spent whole afternoons tanning herself on the already thinning lawn in the garden under the glaring housefront, which shone like a second sun. She liked the sight of the empty lot, a kind of desert which they had all to themselves and which never produced other people. On the morning of July 14, a caravan pitched its site on the other side, near the woods, amid a scene of dust-tossed poppies bathed in red. For a day, Louise took an interest in this unexpected neighbor; sometimes, smoke from a barbecue or the white of a balloon rose from the site. Then she retreated to the solitude of her grief, absorbed in it in total stillness, despite the insects, in the hush of the heat wave where she lived in her bikini. What could her heart be made of to suffer so persistently, so quietly? Benoît found it hard to deal with the quivering sweetness of her naked smile beneath the big dark glasses, and he took to getting on with other things. His mother tried to shake Louise from her torpor but never got anything other than silent tears out of her, which made her sick. She could no longer bear the sight of this wreckage accepted without resistance, and she took out her despair on Vincent, whose presence annoyed her. Her bad faith was total, and Vincent fueled it on purpose. One evening he came home from work with his face smashed in. He had gotten into a fight — no one ever knew why or with whom — and his impatience with the pain of his bruises exacerbated the tension. His parents were coming over the following Sunday, and Vincent must have suddenly felt empowered to claim the right to anger that had been taken from him too soon. Benoît did not like seeing him fretting in the living room like a high-strung, sick animal that wanted to roar but was too afraid of being scolded. In the evening, there were fewer rows with Louise — they would have been far too serious. Vincent's edginess had forced her to get a grip on herself. She now got up at about nine and no longer let the chaos mount up in their room, avoiding any possibility of a clash with Vincent and that ill-stifled sorrow that sought consolation in a fight. One night, Benoît heard them making love; the noise was only just audible, accompanied, or checked, by Louise's murmurs, which were soothing rather than ecstatic, and it ended with a brief gasp, like a man being struck down. It was a very hot Friday and people were setting off on holiday; the throb of engines made it all a bit unreal. Benoît was on the brink of sleep when Louise's murmurs began again with the monotony of a lullaby. He remembered how patient she had been as a mom and was filled with a new sadness, which brought him, at least, the bitter satisfaction of having his share of grief.

Vincent's parents had started out at dawn to beat the traffic jams. They arrived shortly after eleven. Benoît was freeing up a damaged sidecar that was rusting in the jumble of the garage when the car drew up in front of the house. Sweat dripped into his eyes; he felt as though he was seeing the two of them in a mirage. The father wore a summer suit which the long journey had creased up the back, while she was dressed in black and white. They had that awkwardness of people caught out by distress in spite of themselves. Their visit was an act of kindness and despair: they needed, at all cost, if not a culprit (they had given up blaming Louise or Benoît), at least an explanation. So they came humbly, fighting off feelings of guilty irritation with Louise, whom they still loved sincerely, they said, although they had lost heart in this love. Benoît could not bear seeing them so vulnerable. He had never really believed either in their friendliness toward the family or in their modesty about money, and he was embarrassed by their lack of restraint since the accident, compared with their extreme condescension of the old days. He had talked to her a few days earlier on the phone. Her voice sounded exhausted, already with a hint of cowardice at the nightmare of silence she had to face every morning, and Benoît had wanted her to stop talking. The idea that from now on it was every man for himself was starting to take root in him. It all just had to stop.

Benoît gingerly put down his tools so as not to reveal his presence in the garage. His mother ran round from the garden, undoing her apron. She had been to the hairdresser's that morning and seemed not to recognize the feel of her own hair between her fingers. Her haste betrayed the annoyance Louise's confrontation with her parents-in-law caused her—she had not forgotten the difficult scenes of the first evening and now, as then, appeared suspicious and probably unfair toward them. They kissed each other, they very red and she very much on her guard. Louise watched them from the doorstep, shading her eyes with her hand, one foot raised like a heron under her denim skirt. Vincent, who had put on an ironed shirt and washed his hair, held her by the fingertips. In a sense this visit was a good thing, to the extent that it was putting some order back in the life of chaos they had all four been leading for more than a month now.

They had lunch in the garden. Fear of themselves or of their own confusion forced Vincent's parents to be exaggeratedly restrained, and they appeared more relaxed this way, despite the effort they were making. She sat down next to Louise and mothered her with attention. Her mourning seemed to have relaxed with the heat and her puffy face above the white collar looked almost funny. Louise gave diffident answers to her solicitousness as though to a suitor paying court; she was clearly unsure what attitude to adopt and completely incapable of bearing any suffering other than her own. And, as always, when her father-in-law spoke of going to the cemetery, she put her hands over her ears and shut herself off while she waited for him to be quiet.

Summer gripped them in the shimmer from the house walls and the empty lot, but, oddly, no one dared to suggest going in. Vincent would not stop filling their glasses, as if anxious to precipitate upsetting the precarious balance they were in. His jaw was still gray from his bruises, which distorted the expression on his face. Alcohol was making him and his father perspire. Benoît suddenly had the feeling they were going to pounce on him. On the other side of the empty lot, the caravan stood in the shadow of the trees at the edge of summer, and Benoît let his mind wander over to that point. He could make out two slim figures, one of which disappeared among the shadowy trees while the other went along the path with a bucket in either hand. There was a brightly colored curtain at the door and chaise lounges leaning against the caravan.

The little window on the near side was masked by an aluminum panel, which lit up like a headlight every time a breeze bent the trees. Benoît told himself he would go across to it when Vincent's parents had gone.

The coffees were on the table, the shadow of the house descended on them like a soothing hand. The absurd torment of this get-together was coming to an end without having produced anything—no scandal, no comfort. Vincent's nervousness had worn itself out; he was clasping Louise's hand under the table. His father was scarlet and seemed resigned, in spite of himself, to the doom of his grief. When his wife, after scraping the puddle of sugar about at the bottom of her cup for a long moment, spluttered tearfully that she could stand it no more, he brightened up with a brief hope: quite simply, they could leave. He led her aside as though she had committed an indiscretion, and came back a few minutes later to tell them that she was lying on the back seat of the car and that they were off. His voice was toneless, even his anger had gone. Louise stood up, pulling at her tiny tank top to hide her belly-button; she offered him her bed so that he and his wife could rest before they set off. This sudden maturity confused and almost shocked him; he could not figure out this lavish beauty, which was never where he expected it and which must have seemed frustratingly enigmatic to him.

When the car had gone, Vincent came back to the table to empty his glass, and Louise leaned against his shoulder.

The garden was now completely in shadow. Around them, the land crackled like a burning log and grasshoppers creaked hypnotically; a fat lizard burrowed noisily in the pile of dry leaves by the fence. Benoît took another slice of cake. The strain of the meal had given way to the idleness of a scorching Sunday where everything was blurred and wavering. His mother was on the phone; in the silence brought on by digestion they could make out snatches of her coded conversation and, above all, the change in her voice, now false and urgent. Benoît was uneasy, but neither Vincent nor Louise cared what she was saying or to whom she was saying it. They were at peace in the stillness. Vincent had moved away from Louise, whose warmth had made his shirt damp down to the elbow; he seemed absorbed in studying a drunk wasp which was struggling under the tranquil threat of his penknife. Louise was woolgathering, her head resting like a flower on the back of her hand, her eyes lowered, a semi-smile on her lips. What was she thinking about? Benoît did not like seeing her in this state. He asked her what was wrong and in reply she gave a sort of mew but did not open her eyes. It was ages now since they had kissed or confided in one another; Benoît felt he had lost his former love, partly through his own mishandling, and abruptly became hopeless about everything. His mother had hung up but was slow to join them, probably to give herself time to wipe away tears or redness. At the end of the table, Vincent picked his teeth with the point of his deadly penknife and studied the caravan where a yellow canvas awning was opening out. Benoît piled up the plates and they slithered together with a glutinous sound in the remains of the gravy. He needed to air his dejection and suggested going for a walk and, as no one seemed inclined to move, he went off on his bike alone. He waited till he had reached the earth track beside the cornfield to cry.

He was practically at the woods when he saw Vincent coming across the empty lot. He dried his eyes. Vincent was walking quickly toward the caravan, an unlit cigarette clamped between his lips. Everything was shut up. A bath towel had been left out under the awning; only the overwrought voice of a radio was audible from the depths of the trees down by the river. Vincent was now level with Benoît. "They're Dutch," he announced, handing him his cigarette and lighter. "They usually go into the woodcutter's field; I think they're relations of Ilona." There was a tremor of excitement in his voice. Benoît guessed he was in that state of feverishness that was their salvation and the mainstay of their relationship. They walked on side by side in the direction of the reservoir at the edge of the woods. The radio's chatter followed them, working up in them the same unspoken curiosity. Benoît smoked without much pleasure; the cigarette tasted of dirt, but he was happy to be here and already less depressed. His bike jangled like a bell as it bounced over the stones; the noise of the road tucked out of sight behind the sea of tall corn reached them as a muffled drone. Vincent was in conciliatory mood, his aggression over lunch seemed a long way off and almost impossible.

"My parents have asked me to go back and live with them."

The words were spoken like a shot in the country-side and a black veil seemed suddenly to cover Benoît's eyes. When Vincent had thrown his cigarette butt into the undergrowth, he added that there was no question of him going. His voice rang with something approaching hatred. He couldn't stand his father anymore, he admitted after a moment, a man given to violence now tempered and softened by age and the death of the children. Vincent had seen him writhing on his bed one evening, calling for help; Vincent claimed to have said horrible things to him then and would not allow that his father had forgiven him for saying them.

It was the first time Benoît had heard him mention the children's death; he dared not raise his eyes, afraid of having to say something in reply. Vincent cleared his throat and would not stop pushing his hair back, refusing to cry with the obstinate courage of a little boy. Benoît kept pedaling, staring till his head spun at the tire turning under the mudguard. They had come out on the other side of the woods into the full heat of the midafternoon furnace. The babble of the radio was now far behind them, replaced by the echo of water seething against the concrete wall of the reservoir. Vincent had taken hold of himself again, but he kept his face averted. He said he had to go and buy cigarettes and disappeared down a row of corn plants out to the road. Benoît hung around the caravan a bit longer for a change of scene before he went home.

The garden table was cleared and the dishwasher was purring in the kitchen. The wind had scattered petals up to the living room door and the wash looked as though it was floating across the caravan. Benoît put the television on, and it was as he was going to the kitchen to get a piece of cheese that he heard someone groaning upstairs. It was a moan that came from nowhere, and sounded feeble, or, rather, exhausted, as if Louise had been struggling for hours and in vain against her mother's comfort. Benoît went upstairs, avoiding the creaks in the stairs, warmed by the effort. The door was ajar; he pushed it open and saw first the streaks of light from the blinds, then his mother sitting on the bed facing him with an expression that looked already incapable of surprise. Louise was on all fours on the floor; she was not crying, just crawling, begging. It took Benoît a few seconds to realize that she had come for the tranquilizer her mother was stuffing between her lips. He was ashamed of himself. His mother had her hand over her mouth and was watching Louise at her feet, red-eyed but unable to cry. She had no words to console such pain; probably she had not even the first idea of this degree of suffering. Benoît had not moved. Behind him, Vincent was coming upstairs with the agility of a cat; he had some magazines under his arm and stood stock-still on the threshold for a moment. Louise cast him a look of insane hope that must have struck home, for he sat down on the floor beside her and gathered her to him. He hugged her so tightly that his arms shook, and in this embrace that must have hurt her, Louise was gradually soothed. They stayed like this for a long time, tangled together like a fist rocking back and forth; after a while, a sort of crooning rose from them.

When he went into Louise's room in the morning, she was penciling a pearly white line around her puffy eyelids. Her blue eyes smiled at him in the little mirror hanging from the window handle. She was wearing a short, tight-fitting T-shirt that revealed a band of bronze flesh. Her school-girl outfits, which it had never occurred to her to change and which she had always worn without a second thought, gave her grief a heartrending sincerity. The sun ricocheted off the mirror and cast an illusory brightness over her face; Louise was fading away and her efforts made no difference. Benoît was filled with a terrible nostalgia for her happiness, her free spirit. She carefully replaced the cap on the eyeliner, then perched on one thigh on the edge of the windowsill where she sat and watched him. Her belly-button protruded provocatively over the waist-band of her skirt; Benoît found her irresistible. She smiled, told him he was handsome and with adorable grace laid a finger on her own lips then on his, a gesture she seemed to unearth from the depths of her memory of another life. Benoît was in love and unhappy, the most unbearable part being that Louise was trying to fool them all, not for her own sake but for theirs, already aware, with the insight that came from her kindness, that her grief had become a burden to them.

A door slammed downstairs. Louise felt for her sandals with her toes and wriggled her feet into them. A cloud glided out of the trees and cast a shadow on the house behind her. Louise put one of Vincent's shirts over her tiny T-shirt. Benoît watched her loosen the soft waves of her hair from the collar then patiently roll up the sleeves, which were too long on her. He dared not kiss her; she had become an object of fear and respect, something it was painful to love.

Vincent had already left; their mother was very late. Her bad temper immediately distracted them from their melancholy. She gave Louise a few instructions, and Louise reacted to her irritability with a curious pursing of her lips as though trying to restrain a burst of laughter, then she went out of the room without even shutting the door behind her. A gust of wind swept down the hallway and blew open the French door to the garden with a rattle of locks and panes. It grew dark suddenly. Louise went to cut a slice of bread and butter and ate it sitting on the garden steps. The sky was disappearing in a sort of trail of clouds that took with it whole flocks of birds. Benoît eyed the caravan furtively; it stood on the edge of their horizon, looking self-contained, very white and abandoned. The memory of their curiosity, his and Vincent's, when they heard the distant sound of the radio among the trees, filled him with vague remorse. He told himself he would spend the day with Louise, a prospect that made him both depressed and happy.

Until eleven the weather remained undecided, with disorderly clouds careening about, fading or bursting into flame in a blade-like ray of sun. Benoît was mending the hi-fi speakers in the living room. Louise had swapped Vincent's shirt for a big cable-stitch sweater that splayed out over her hips. Tidying the house and getting lunch for her brother had put a bit of life back into her. The thick soles of her sandals weighed down her lanky figure as she moved about with the noise of a horse's hooves. She lived only through the pleasure of serving other people; Benoît realized that this was maybe what was needed to cure her. The stillness together with the distant voices carrying across on the wind from the caravan caused him an impatience he found almost pleasant. Louise had made spaghetti; she ate squatting on her heels on the floor by the sofa, her hair tangled against the velvety cushions. She talked about Vincent, said that he was planning to get a motorbike. Her tolerance toward him was an endless source of generosity. She was unusually talkative, describing details of her life at her parents-in-laws' and showing the fascination of a child unaccustomed to luxuries like the round bathtub and off-white carpets. Benoît panicked momentarily as he sensed her coming so close to mentioning the children, but Louise was happy and carefree this morning. He thought she was amazing to let her mind be taken off immeasurable despair by recalling a midnight-blue washbasin or the big painted mirror in her bedroom. He adored her.

Then the sun came back out, the summer sky seemed suddenly petrified, and the heat began to rise. Louise took off her sweater and threw her sandals across the room. Her skin felt moist against Benoît's arm and her breath fluttered on his cheek. It was mildly uncomfortable being this close. Louise was silent. She fiddled absently with the hem of her skirt and watched the dazzling sunlight lay siege to the door. Dust from the cushions rose like a wall between them. A fat black fly was peacefully drinking the remains of the Bolognaise sauce, which was starting to give off a cloying smell. Louise took the plates out and came and sat back down a bit further away on the sofa. She put her hand on Benoît's thigh, but the charm was broken. Their mother was late coming home; having to wait for her made it impossible to do anything else. Benoît would have liked to go out but felt bound by his promise to give his time to Louise. She had put the television on and spread her hair over the sofa back to air her neck. It was at once excruciating and pleasant sitting still like this. Benoît was touched by the sacrifice he had agreed to. It occurred to him that Elodie might be back from her grandparents', and this thought gave the day a kind of meaning.

Their mother came home partway through the afternoon looking haggard from lack of sleep. She glanced briefly at Louise and beckoned to Benoît to come into the kitchen. He found her rinsing off the abandoned plates in the sink, cross that nothing had been done, that everything was heavy and painful. "How is she?" she asked, nodding her chin at the living room. She did not expect the truth, just an answer with which they could hope to go on living. Irritation and despair in her were about evenly balanced. Then she asked what time Vincent had got up, and when Benoît said he had no idea, her mouth assumed an odd expression of scorn. The floor tiles began to shudder with the rumble of the dishwasher. Benoît did not know if he should go out or stay in; he resented his mother for only partially sharing her worries and adding to the tension. Louise had not moved from the sofa; possibly she had not even noticed her brother go out. Everything seemed pointless; Benoît had never felt so downcast. Outside, nature stood still in the blistering afternoon sun. The caravan had barricaded itself against the surrounding desert. It was too hot to tinker in the garage, so Benoît went upstairs to his room. The curtains were drawn, little patches of light flickered about the room like fireflies. He turned on the radio and lay down on his bed. Almost immediately he heard a knock at the door and saw Louise's face appear in the doorway. Her face was still marked by creases from the sofa. She was coming to say that he mustn't worry about her and should just go out if he wanted. She had approached cautiously, as though anxious she might not recognize him. Perspiration had erased the eyeliner and her eyes look even paler and softer. She was stunningly beautiful; Benoît was cross with himself for doing as she said.

When he went out at about five, Louise was in the kitchen with her mother. A sizzling pan drowned their conversation, or rather the suppressed cries of his mother, who was overwrought with lassitude and grief. There was starting to be a bit of air and traffic on the road. Benoît went to fetch his bike from the garage and rode off along the main road in the filthy slipstream of a trailer truck; the physical effort pleasantly lifted his spirits. He had some trouble finding Elodie's parents' house among the scattered hedges and silence in this district, which summer had left to itself. The shutters were closed; a big rose bush reached out a purple sucker of soft leaves that were like skin. The morning rain had cast dirt over the short driveway up to the front steps and crushed the pretty, poisonous berries on the bushes. Benoît wished he had not come. This day was making him increasingly depressed; he could not even bring himself to go into the town center to see if anyone was around. As he was heading back to the main road, at the roundabout exit, he noticed Vincent's car parked at the roadside.

The dull thudding of the transistor radio poured out into the silent fields through the wide-open doors. Vincent was smoking, toying with the torn leather on the steering wheel. He did not seem very surprised to see Benoît and told him he had pretended he had an appointment at the dentist's to get away before closing time. He was getting sick of this work, he let out with a nod at the bike, which Benoît had dropped in the grass. His eyes shone with unusual intensity. Benoît was pleased to see him; he was not very nice with his offhand manners of an only son, but he was pleasant to be around, mostly because this same behavior restored a bit of levity to existence. As evening fell, flocks of sparrows came swooping into the corn. Vincent had gotten out of his seat to sit in the grass next to Benoît and he drew dreamily on his cigarette, resting his head against the seat. After a moment, a truck drew up beside them, filling the car with the noise of the engine and the stink of exhaust fumes. The driver's genial face peered at them through the little window in the door; Vincent yelled at him to push off out of it and sounded his horn, scattering the sparrows and field mice hidden in the convolvulus. The incident put them in a good mood. Vincent brought out a can of warm beer; the foam frothed over his hands. They both took a long swig, and sweat broke out instantly on their foreheads. Vincent talked about his boss, whom he thought uninspiring, and about a plan to open a shop in September with a mysterious pal Benoît had never heard him mention before. Then, suddenly, his face clouded. He peered into the distance, a stubborn look in his close-set eyes, that feature that meant he would never be handsome despite his thick black hair and good figure. When he had finished the beer and crushed the can between his knees, he asked Benoît if he had spoken to his mother since the morning. He seemed to have placed considerable hope in this question and it bothered him for several minutes. Benoît understood why the following week.

He had gone to join a friend who was fishing for eels using a stocking stuffed with maggots. Standing still in the chilly water flowing under the bent branches of wild roses had numbed him through, and he had gone back up the hot, sun-bleached meadow to a little wooden hut where there were often coins to be found. It was a windowless fisherman's hut half-buried among the branches, and it took Benoît a few seconds to make out, through what remained of the door, a pair of buttocks splayed like a fruit on a wide and rosy looking anus, then almost immediately Vincent's flushed face emerging directly above it. He signaled to Benoît to scram—the girl had hardly moved her head from his prick, which she was manipulating a bit indifferently—and Benoît bolted. Blood warmed his cheeks like nettle stings. He despised himself for being so aroused. His boots caught in the long grass of the meadow, sending out a spray of pollen and insects. When he got to the river, he slid under the thorns into a sodden, mossy hideaway. Creepers dangled among the algae swaying at the surface, making a lapping sound that tortured his bladder and his erection, and he thought he would never manage to come before Vincent had finished with the girl.

When the surprise of pleasure was over, deafening him for a few moments to the roar of cascading water just at his feet, he did up his fly and tried to make out what was going on in the hut. Soon, he heard the slow squelch of feet wading up the river and saw the figure of his pal coming into view in a cloud of insects under the canopy of bushes. He was off, now, and Benoît told him not to wait, so the other boy poked his way through the branches, his bag on his hip. Benoît waited until he had disappeared before climbing out into the light. Vincent had gone to look for him a bit further up the road; they came back together near the hut.

Vincent immediately declared that he had asked the girl to go away, then, as though this explained something, that it was the girl from the caravan and that she did not know about the children. He had sat down with his back to the wooden wall and kept gently knocking his head against it, and, although Benoît had said nothing, having not even had time to think anything at all, he worked himself up into a sort of uncontrollable rage. His voice was raised and he kept wiping his eyes with his fist, repeating over and over that no one here was really in a position to tell him what was right or not and that anyway Louise had stopped wanting to make love and that she had never really done it properly. Benoît stared down between his feet and made no move, uneasy at Vincent's distress. The wooden hut felt rough against his shoulder blades, his boots stank of river mud. He said he was resentful, less with Vincent than for the way circumstances had worked out: by taking his children away life had somehow given Vincent a second chance.

Vincent looked disheveled and this evidence made his confusion all the more poignant. He was silent now but his tears and nose would not stop running. It was the first time since the accident that Benoît had seen him cry, the first time, too, that he had realized how little point there was to him staying with them. He felt sorry for him and was a bit jealous, but not for a second did he think that it was an insult to Louise, as if his heart had never really grasped the full facts of the matter. Vincent had got up to straighten his clothes. Benoît asked him how his mother knew, and he answered that she had come across him talking to the girl by the road and that she hated him enough to guess the rest. His jaw clicked open and shut like an overwound mechanical toy. Benoît had never suspected that Vincent might be sensitive to his mother's hostility. In that instant, when circumstances could scarcely have been less appropriate, he realized that Vincent was the only friend he had left.

It was the following Monday when Vincent received the money from his parents. Benoît saw his mother open the door to the postman shortly before midday and place the little pile of bills where they would be seen on the sideboard. When Vincent came in from work he immediately told Benoît and Louise to come up to his room so he could show them the amount; it seemed unthinkable. Louise glanced at the bundle in cautious delight, marveling at so much money. In the curtainless room, darkening with the rosy glow of evening, she looked like a child under a spell. Vincent promised that they would buy a motorbike and go and spend some time on the south coast with Benoît. Louise looked at them both as though they were magicians, her hands flat against her cheeks, which were quivering slightly. Their mother had the week off work; she had not made a single remark but doubtless considered that the amount was obscene, or at least irresponsible. Their excitement must hurt her; she probably felt she had the strength neither to tolerate nor to combat the idleness of the three of them this whole summer, and her silent reproach made the secret pleasure of the moment keener. Louise went back to daydreaming. She saw Vincent as a kind of charmed thief. Benoît imagined that loving him like this would make her happy again. Added to which, for three days after the money came, Vincent never left her side, holding her tightly in his hands as though to squeeze out the sap, warm the dull flesh back to life. He gave her a big ring, and she looked at it gratefully and put it away safely in a little box. Indeed, the possibilities offered by this windfall seemed to grant them a reprieve, an impression the fine weather somehow confirmed. It was not yet too hot; the empty lot was strewn with the flowers and sweet wrappers that blew across toward the woods with the insects. The caravan and its yellow awning had become part of the scene; Vincent took no more notice of it. Perhaps it was the feel of the money in his pocket, perhaps it was remorse, but he seemed content just to be kind to Louise.

Vincent was set on his idea of buying a motorbike, in need of a project to stave off the anxiety of having a summer of silence to fill. For a few days they went around the dealers in the area, and it was on the way back from one of these trips that Vincent came up with the idea of teaching Benoît to drive. He turned off on to the hardened ruts of a country road and handed over the steering wheel. Behind them, Louise surrounded the two seatbacks with her love. She was chewing gum and Benoît could hear it squeak then burst by his ear. The wheel was hot in his hands, the strain of driving held his head in a vice. Beside him, Vincent kept both hands on his thighs to stop them shaking; nothing seemed able to contain his impatience. A bare hundred yards away, the constant drone of the main road thundering through the clefts in the landscape was an irresistible incitement to Benoît to accelerate. Vincent told him once to slow down; Louise laughed with pleasure at the unfamiliar tone of his voice. She had leaned her cheek against the seatback and twined her fingers within Vincent's. Her love for him, that enduring adolescent passion, was one of the charms to which she had the key. The road continued very close to the river's edge as though about to tip into the bushes trailing in the water. The reflection of Louise's face trembled in the rearview mirror; she had closed her eyes and was humming a song, hardly moving her lips. Her fingers clasped in Vincent's were turning white. Benoît was glad to see her relax. The sensation of speed was increased by the vibrations from the ruts and the car threw up dust which all but masked the brambled slopes blocking the road behind them. Benoît's jaw ached from so much concentration and repressed exhilaration, and when Vincent yelled at him to slow down, he did not even have the instinct to obey. Vincent shot him a look of panic that made him swerve to the side. They felt the weeds and branches scraping against the chassis of the car then the back wheel jump and jam in the ditch between the road and the fields. Vincent bellowed that they really were completely insane and spat on the ground to purge a burst of hatred, which he must have known was out of proportion. He leaped out of the car muttering that they needn't be surprised now about what had happened; Louise leaned forward to see the expression on his face. Her teeth had left a little purple line on her lip; she hung on to Benoît's arm to stop him, too, from leaving her.

Vincent was already more than ten yards along the path, his shoulder blades shrugging under his shirt where damp patches had spread under the arms. Tears of apologetic astonishment began to blur Louise's eyes. Benoît felt mortified and guilty toward her for what Vincent had said. He pressed his face to hers in a moment of shared tenderness that was warm and salty. Around them the wind rummaged among the stalks, scattering birds from the meadows. Benoît told her he loved her very much, and she replied that she loved him very much too; then, seeing him about to add something, she clenched her fists and closed her eyes in a silent prayer for him not to say anything. When they opened their eyes, Vincent was coming back to the car, throwing gravel at the windscreen. He had calmed down and in fact looked very upset by what had just happened and wanted to be forgiven. Indeed, it was hard to believe how attentive he was. Louise leaned over the seat to kiss him, a long, slow kiss with her tongue that made a lapping sound in the silence of the car. Benoît no longer knew if he should be glad or cry; this idle August suddenly seemed fraught with danger to him.

It must have been about seven and they had only just gotten back, when Vincent was called by his parents. They had already tried to get ahold of him twice on previous days; Vincent replied (probably to their reproaches) with disagreeable mumbles, giving Benoît to understand that the couple had succumbed to the panic of emptiness and were asking Vincent and Louise to spend the end of the summer in the south. Perhaps in sending the money they had hoped to tempt Louise with the memory of the comforts of a little princess, as though offering her candy. Their solitude must have reached that point of cruelty where nothing else matters, not even other people's happiness. Benoît went to join his mother in the kitchen to avoid overhearing the feeble excuses Vincent was coming out with to put them off. She made him tell her what she had already guessed herself: Vincent's parents were demanding Louise back. Heat from the oven and indignation at their egoism contorted her face. Benoît took a boiling potato out of the pan; his heart sank at the thought that Louise and Vincent might go. His mother still said nothing, fully determined not to let her daughter sink deeper into her memories, but holding back her reaction and refusal for a call she intended to make in secret to Vincent's parents late that night or early the next morning. Benoît thought her resistance fair but that it didn't make her very nice. She was almost ugly when she was cross, and this thought consoled him in his frustration at her refusal to share her worries with him. The potato's grainy heat covered his palate. He wondered if his mother still thought about loving them.

Vincent had hung up; he took Louise by a finger and led her into a corner of the garden. Benoît watched them from the kitchen window. The sun was very low behind the tall electricity pylons and cast a shadow of crisscross lines over them. Louise followed the movements of Vincent's lips with obedient concentration. There was a burst of motorbike engines over by the caravan and Vincent glanced up briefly. He was scratching his shoulder, keeping his eyes on the ground as he talked; Louise's attention seemed to be bothering him. For a few seconds Benoît was sure they were going to leave. His mother was busy setting the table, clattering the knives and forks roughly together with an unbearable jangle. She had her back to the door when Vincent came in. He told her that he was going away for a few days but on his own, and she nodded an acknowledgment by way of thanking him. Louise hovered in the doorway and stared at her, smiling, barely interested in what had been decided for her. She had just brushed her hair and it clung around her neck with static electricity. Benoît was worried about the solitude that awaited them; Vincent's outburst against them just now in the car had stirred them to the very depths of their being.

When Benoît got up the next day, there was a smell of disinfectant downstairs and Louise was reading in the garden. She still seemed unconcerned by Vincent's approaching departure. Benoît took a chaise lounge and placed it beside hers. They chatted for a few minutes. Louise had shut her magazine; her cheek was flattened against the canvas and her speech sounded numbed. She was not really listening now, lulled by her brother's presence into a peaceful state of well-being. Benoît saw her against the light: her arm cast a small shadow; a vaccination scar formed a pink wound among the light downy hairs; the stubble growing back in the crook of her armpit was shiny with sweat or deodorant. Her smells were all acrid with faintly sugary undertones and there was a slight yeasty sourness on her breath; now and again her relaxed body gave a long gurgle. As Benoît had stopped talking, she smiled a melancholy smile at him, then turned her face to the caravan where the yellow awning had been folded up. Benoît asked where Vincent was, and Louise told him with a broad sweep of her arm that he had gone to see someone in town. Then there was a silence. Louise had dozed off in spite of the teasing insects hovering around a clump of pincushion flowers which the wind had sown beside the fence. When he craned his neck, Benoît could see the car's red roof over the heap of scrap metal. Vincent was on foot; Benoît reckoned he must have set off nearly an hour ago. His mother was talking in lowered tones on the phone in the hall; it was as though an invisible plot was being woven around Louise as she slept. Benoît felt immense, powerless love for her. She had turned her head in her sleep; a thick, chalky trickle of saliva emphasized her sleepwalker's half-smile. Benoît was struck by it: Louise was not asleep but stunned by her tranquilizers, which brought her an other-worldly peace, a peace as foamy as this line on her lips. He got up, distressed and embarrassed at happening upon his sister's mildly distasteful secrets, suddenly suspecting a flaw in her beauty lying cast up on the chaise lounge. His mother had gone out without even telling him. Vincent's long absence was starting to pall. He felt defenseless beside Louise, whom it seemed nothing should wake, as though she were some precious object which it was up to him to guard, alone and unarmed. He went to the fence to scan the horizon, expecting to see Vincent emerge any minute from the swathes of pale green corn. Behind him,

Louise's sleep made no noise, not even a hint. Benoît felt oppressed. He went to the bathroom to splash himself with water. The drafts played on his nerves and seemed to shake the house. So he went upstairs to stare out the window at the road, at this hour all but deserted.

The tall buildings in the town center now formed no more than a single block in the dazzling brightness, a white screen where the tiny dot of Vincent's figure soon appeared and grew with the magic of a mirage. When he drew level with the car, Vincent did up his shoelace and checked the contents of the cigarette packet in his shirt pocket. Benoît threw the cap of a beer bottle at him, and he dodged it with a smile that was rather silly and self-congratulatory but agreeable too. He had probably gone to look for the caravan girl, as though checking up on a possession. Benoît was not even offended; already he had lost all idea of what was right or wrong.

His mother arrived a few seconds after Vincent; she said she had seen him in the tobacco shop, neither cross nor taken in about the real reason for his escapade to town and at most intrigued as to what he was up to. She must have known Louise was too immature to make a childless marriage last long, and she was sensible enough to realize that you couldn't blame anyone for the consequences. Vincent was careful with her by being attentive to Louise, and this arrangement was the best thing that had happened to them in a long while.

Louise woke up at last. She hesitated for a moment on the edge of the chaise lounge then took a long drink to slake the sickly thirst she did not even know she had. Vincent was sitting on the ground at her feet, watching her through eyes half closed by the sun. He was in a good mood and said that he had heard about a nearly new, secondhand motorbike. Louise gave a cheery little "oh!" but Benoît could see she had not been listening.

Vincent had planned to leave the next afternoon—he wanted to arrive at his parents' late, as though to accustom them from the outset to the frustration of having him around—and he devoted the whole of the last day to Louise and Benoît, apparently hoping to make up for his liaison by depriving the caravan girl of his company.

They had got up early to go and see the motorbike at a mechanic's whose workshop abutted the sawmill a couple of miles up from the gravel pit. The weather was unsettled; all night they had heard the garden fence rattling and the booming metal sheeting of the garage as it bellowed in and out. Vincent had brought the car round to the door to wait for Louise; he asked Benoît if she was all right, and Benoît said "yes," partly because he had not thought about it. The wind whistled through the chinks in the car, and they sat in silence the whole time as they waited for Louise to appear, watching the contortions of a newspaper trapped by a stone. She took a long time getting ready, but Benoît noticed straight away that she had not washed before putting on her makeup. A little yellow residue had built up in the corner of her carefully penciled eye, and her neck was streaked with salt just under her ear. It was astonishing; he felt terribly sad.

Louise made them tell her again where they were going—she seemed only just to have realized—then she inserted a tape, patiently unfastened her sandals, and put her feet against the windscreen. Speed finally brought her back to them, and she was almost cheerful by the time Vincent turned off along a dirt road thick with garage waste and which came to an end at the low wall of a little sluice below the workshop. High elder bushes had sprouted in the damp from the pool and screened the place from the sun and road. Louise glanced gingerly into the cesspool's mossy depths; a trickle of oily water seeped out through a deep crack by the hedge. She shivered in her long lacy, white woolen cardigan, which clung around her bare legs under the denim skirt like a sock. Benoît hugged her to him; she pressed her face into his neck and said that it gave her a funny feeling being here.

Vincent had gone to meet the mechanic who was already bringing the motorbike into the sun. Louise followed at a cautious distance and nodded a greeting to the man, then came back to the car. Vincent crouched down beside the machine as though by an invalid, and stroked a finger over it, casting enigmatic glances at Benoît from time to time. Down by the pool, the car radio had started to splutter a few notes, followed by a loud crackling and finally an almost recognizable tune. Louise stood with her back to them, her arms flat on the hood, her long thighs under the white knitted cardigan together, like hands in prayer, and swaying in time to the music. Benoît would have liked to go and wait with her but was too afraid of not showing enough interest in the bike. The man intimidated him; he must have known his father in the days of the service station, and he presumably knew about the children for he kept looking inquiringly at the three of them.

They left after a quarter of an hour, once Vincent had tried out the motorbike on the woodchips from the sawmill and jotted down the workshop number on the back of his hand. The man came out a few paces along the path, as though to check that they were really on their way. His figure seemed to melt into the blue opacity of the elder bushes as they withdrew. Benoît said to himself that Louise must have made a surprisingly good impression, unless he thought he had mistaken her for somebody else. Even Benoît at that moment could not believe that she had had children, that she had seen them die, and that it was killing her.

Vincent even took them into town for a beer. He was on edge at the thought of getting a good bargain. Louise would not stop kissing him; no one suspected that she had taken it into her head to leave with him.

They were in the hall. Vincent already had his bag over his shoulder and Louise was blocking his exit, sitting on the floor with her arms around her knees as though trussed up in her cardigan. She did not want to stay here without Vincent, and it was true: probably, she could not be happy anywhere, life flayed her wherever she put herself, and this torment, which she had never mentioned, had grown sadly impossible to share. The noise of a tractor grinding up the barely perceptible slope alongside the house partly drowned her sobs. Her mother listened to her fighting for breath for a few seconds, clearly distressed at this new trauma, then made a lunge to pull her up by one arm the way she would have hauled on a strap, but, failing to make any impact, she uttered the bizarre threat of calling a doctor. Louise cast a horrified glance at Benoît, her eyes swimming with tears, but he was no more able to explain this outburst of severity than she. Probably she still did not fully believe Vincent's determination, for she jumped like a startled animal when he pushed her aside to try to get out. She shuddered feverishly in the evening heat. Vincent had opened all the car doors to get rid of the stink of synthetic covers and pick up the crumpled chewing gum wrappers and empty cans from their recent excursions. His indifference to what she might be attempting made her cry more bitterly and spurred her to make a sudden dash to go and sit in the car. She was acting faintly ridiculous, but Benoît could not help thinking that she was right. Her shoulder blades stuck up like two little wings on her despairing figure, and when Vincent's shadow approached her on the parking lot she seemed to shrink still further into herself like a snail. He was not unkind to her, and he must have felt sorry at this preposterous situation, for he showed no brutality as he tried to pull her toward him. But when she felt him touch her, Louise began to sob so horribly that, in a fit of panic, Vincent seized her head in both hands and shook it, shouting till she stopped, not calmed but stunned. Benoît could no longer stand seeing her manhandled, her face smeared with snot and tears. She was staring fixedly in front of her, still clinging to the seat, then suddenly, probably barely conscious of what he was doing, Vincent grasped her around the waist and picked her out of the car like a log. Benoît yelled that he was hurting her and ran into the kitchen, kicking open the doors. A trickle of saltwater dribbled down his throat. He heard his mother's voice through the air vent above the sink, then a loud hoot as Vincent drove off the parking lot, and, not long after, just over his head, Louise's steps going upstairs to take refuge in her room. Benoît hesitated briefly before going up to her, weakly hanging back, unable to tell scruples from pity. His mother was sitting on the stairs; she told him to come down and tell her when the two of them had calmed down.

He found Louise in bed, her back wedged against the wall. In spite of the heat, she had pulled the sheet up to her shoulders over her cardigan and was staring stubbornly at the woods. Benoît did not like seeing her behave incomprehensibly; he had the sickening feeling that everything was falling apart. The window shook in the wind, causing a crooked star shape to flicker over the wall; Louise made a childish gesture to catch it, then let out a murmur that it would have been better if she had died. It was wisely said: quite simply, Louise was beginning to know she was too much. Benoît felt guilty for having so quickly and cowardly turned away from her distress. He crouched down and pressed his head against her through the soft quilt. She stroked his hair and turned down a corner of the sheet, letting out a waft of her fruity perfume mingled with the smell of the couple's nights together. Downstairs in the garden their mother was folding up the chaise lounges, which snapped to like sticks, then she coughed, shut the French window, and finally came upstairs to see what was going on. She had taken off her apron; the smell of the wash was still on her hands, and her fingers were wrinkled from the water. She sat down at the end of the bed and shook Louise's foot through the quilt as though to get a smile out of her. Louise wore an expression of pity and unspeakable gratitude, then suddenly, without a word, she pushed off the covers and let them see her thighs; they were clawed till they bled, and her hands lay inert on either side: two weapons abandoned at the scene of the crime. A piece of pink skin was stuck under her pointed nails; the cardigan and sheets were spattered with blood. It seemed incredible that someone could do themselves so much harm in this way. Louise did not move, a bit confused at revealing her wretchedness like this. Her mother never left off smiling, perhaps trying to minimize the seriousness of what she had done, and Benoît got up to let her take his place, feeling obscurely that the situation demanded experience. Louise recoiled slightly in the bed, and her mother seized her chin and searched her face for a long time, as though the solution to their unhappiness lay there, under her nose.

Benoît went down to the kitchen. He was hungry but everything made his stomach churn. The window had darkened and above the outline of the woods the tops of the tall trees looked as though they were being blown to pieces. There was a rumble, then a rolling sound, and almost immediately the caravan's yellow awning began to flap like a sail, held at one end by two slim figures, one of which must be the girl. Benoît had the wild idea that Vincent might have been over there while Louise was scratching the skin off her thighs in their bed, and had this been the case, he told himself, he was not sure he could have blamed him.

A white plastic bag whipped across the garden into the fence where it caught and snagged with a loud crackling. Benoît had finally decided on a peach; the juice dribbled down his chin. He felt almost nothing now; it was a shame but that was how it was: his conscience was deserting him. The French window was just pulled to, and he jumped as he sensed his mother come up behind him. She leaned on the fence, made a move to put her arm around him, then abandoned the idea. The wounds weren't that bad, she said, best not to tell Vincent about it. Her hands still smelled of the wash and her face was a bit shiny. She was silent. The two small figures continued to wrestle with the canvas awning at the edge of the field. Benoît thought his mother was going to talk about Vincent's affair, but it was something else that was bothering her: she wanted to know if he would agree to stay in with his sister that evening.

She was going out. Benoît was lost for an answer. It was arranged a long time ago, she added, pursing her lips with pointless aggression. She stared at the distant caravan among the trees, which were swaying with tremendous force. A tear she could never wipe away was welling in the corner of her eye. Yet Benoît knew she was not sad, just stubborn. Above them, Louise coughed in her sleep. Benoît guessed his mother had given her a tranquilizer, the way she always did when there was nothing else to do.

He did not even blame her, thinking, simply, that they had become disgustingly pragmatic. His mother still dared not go and get ready, but her attention already seemed to have wandered a long way from Louise through a sort of healthy resignation that enabled her to put up with the whole thing. She braced herself at last, as though taking the weight of the world on her shoulders, and went in picking up a stray fork that was sticking up out of the grass. Louise coughed again, a nasty, phlegmy cough, the plastic bag thrashed against the stakes of the fence, and the dense roll of clouds over the woods was lit for a few seconds by the last rays of the sun, like a projector aimed at the house.

Benoît threw himself on the couch in front of the TV; he felt sick that there was no letup or escape for him, either, sometimes. His mother shouted to him from the bathroom that there were some leftover chicken and ratatouille he could heat up, but he made no answer. He heard her come and go, then drop a powder compact that broke on the tiled floor. Her perfume wafted through the door and out into the evening air. Benoît leaned to one side to watch her. She had put on a sleeveless dress that showed the damp, pudgy flesh around her carefully shaved armpits. The white roots of her dyed blond hair were already growing out and struck an odd contrast with her immaculate makeup. Benoît saw her rummage among the shoes in the cupboard under the stairs, slip on a pair of fancy sandals, and hobble back into the bathroom. She took no notice of him, formidably intent on her decision and selfishness. Benoît was hungry but he was reluctant to interrupt her preparations, which cost both of them so dearly.

The doorbell rang for the first time just as he was getting up to fetch a glass of water. His mother rushed toward the living room door to stop him going to answer it. "Don't go, he thinks you've gone to stay with Louise. He doesn't know about the children," she brought out in an undertone, sounding strangely annoyed, almost threatening. Benoît took a few seconds to understand what she meant. He could not get over how she could have kept quiet about such a tragedy and be so terrified of it, while at the same time he had got to the point of admitting that his mother did not want to put her affair in jeopardy by souring it with a death. The bell rang again but she did not immediately go and open the door, wanting to make sure first that Benoît would not give her away, that he had fully understood that her happiness, her last pleasures, which she deserved, were at stake. Her expression was awesome. Benoît felt a sense of admiration and mild disgust that had nothing to do with her, or very little. At that moment he was convinced that it was just plain inevitable.

Vincent called at about ten. He had just gotten back; it had taken him less than four hours. His voice still shook with the thrill of speed and freedom that had warmed his body, that feeling of being alive which Benoît realized for the first time he felt denied. Vincent wanted to know how Louise was. His concern was genuine, and Benoît answered that she was in bed but that he thought he had heard her move. Sure enough, she appeared by the banisters. She had taken off her skirt but left on her white cardigan; her hipbones stuck out just enough to stretch the thin elastic of her panties; her sores were now puffy on her thighs. Benoît found nothing more to say to Vincent. Louise took the receiver he was holding out to her, carefully tucked her hair behind her ear and asked in a whisper who it was. Benoît could see her face reflected in the hall mirror, her downcast eyes with their red rings. The conversation lasted a few minutes. Louise gave barely audible "yes" and "no" answers to what must have been promises or words of consolation. Her smile was one of absolute grace. Benoît noticed that the tranquilizers had dried her mouth out again and that her tongue stuck around the words. When she had finished, she replaced the receiver with both hands and went to join Benoît in the living room. She was hungry and her feet were cold, she said, drawing her knees up under her T-shirt. Benoît went to get her the remains of the chicken and ratatouille, and she ate it hungrily. She smelled of cold cream and an unwashed body, and her cheeks shone with face cream in the TV light. She told him what Vincent had said, insisting in a voice full of sympathy that her parents-in-law did not sound very well, and Benoît wondered if she maybe did not realize what a bad way she was in herself. Outside, the continual threat of rain was worrying the insects, which they could hear thudding against the glass like pellets. A last ribbon of light lingered behind the trees. Louise went to draw the curtains and came hopping back to her place in front of the TV. They sat holding hands all evening watching a horror movie, fascinated, and it was not until a few minutes before their mother came home that Louise appeared to notice her absence.

They had heard neither the car nor the keys in the lock, just the noise of the umbrella being dropped on to the hall stand. She was surprised to find both of them there; she had the breathless manner of someone rushing in to avert a catastrophe. Louise shouted to her that Vincent had called. The scars on her legs belied her cheerful tone, but her mother seemed not to want to worry about her for the moment. She changed her shoes but left her date dress on and came and sat down next to them on the sofa. Benoît stiffened slightly at the feel of her bare arms, now with the smell of an unfamiliar soap on them. She asked if they had eaten and what they were watching. Her feet toyed absently with a corner of the rug, she could not stop yawning, and finally fell asleep. At the first snore, Louise leaned toward her and gave her brother's leg a discreet pinch. She was hardly surprised to learn that her mother was having an affair; she even had an indulgent twinkle in her eye.

There was a distant flash of lightning, and almost immediately they were plunged in darkness by a power cut, though the fluorescent television screen continued to glow in front of them for a few seconds. When the lights came back on, their mother had woken up and was on her feet. She suggested they go to bed. Benoît went on watching the end of a film on another channel, and when he went up in his turn, his mother was with Louise. He heard her talking to her for some time, too quietly for him to make out the words, then he went into his room and locked the door. He was not tired. The storm had rumbled off, leaving a steamy, electric atmosphere hanging over the area. The warm bed linens made his skin itch. At about one o'clock he went out to go for a ride. The wind cast a damp veil over his face. He cycled fifty yards or so across the empty lot; the thin beam of his front light jiggled randomly among the bumps, finally disturbing a cat which slunk off to glare through the dark with its glittering eyes somewhere else. Benoît stopped but could still hear his saddle squeaking in the silence. Louise's window lit up for a fraction of a second, then Benoît turned back. Indoors, all was quiet. He hesitated a moment, listening outside Louise's door, wanting to go in but not daring. His love for her was the only thing that had made him so happy and so unhappy.

Benoît got to know the caravan girl a few days later. She was emptying a steaming bucket of water over the nettles. Benoît recognized her auburn hair, the ends bleached by the sun, and the indifferent expression she had worn in the hut when she looked up from between Vincent's thighs. She must have recognized him, too, because she called out a vaguely ironic greeting to him, keeping her eyes on the upturned bucket. Benoît cycled on, his heart beating stupidly fast. The day was coolish; rain had fallen during the night, and dust from the country road stuck to his wheels. Benoît was already at the edge of the woods; the branches were still spangled with water droplets, and he shivered uneasily. Behind him, the track was deserted and the caravan, with its coating of tree debris and patches of rust, looked chilly. Benoît sought an excuse to turn around. Vincent was due back in a couple of days; his absence was starting to pall. Louise was resigned to it in her semi-conscious way; Benoît dared barely admit to himself that he was getting bored in her company. His mother had taken another week off work. Louise's destructive outburst had given her a shock, but she had registered it only by degrees, as if she needed to get used to this new dimension to their plight one step at a time. She got her to help with the housework more often and took her shopping in town for whole mornings. Louise obediently mimicked her mother's energy. Left to himself, Benoît had started mending the sidecar with the help of a pal who was on his own this summer and was more bored than the rest of them. Gradually, life was returning to normal and Benoît tried to be happy; all he felt now was a greedy impatience to see daylight again.

A gust of wind shook the water from the branches, then an animal rustled among the dead wood in the bushes. Benoît had the feeling the girl was close by. He could not make up his mind to go home. The late morning sun was pleasantly warming this part of the scenery, and in the distance the house cast its narrow shadow in the direction of the caravan. From where he stood, they did not seem so far apart; Benoît could even see that his mother and Louise had gone indoors by the puff of steam escaping through the vent in the kitchen. He was seeing the house from a different angle and it gave him a funny feeling, like looking at a mirror image of his life. What would become of them when school started? Panic seized him unexpectedly in the pit of his stomach and his feet skidded off the pedals. He looked up at the road and it seemed to shimmer momentarily before his eyes. It must be nearly midday; Benoît told himself he had just time to go back to the caravan before lunch. His wheel gave a springy lurch over a fat slug and he watched it shrink in the mud before slithering away.

He first made out the smell of boiled vegetables and burning coal, then he noticed the back of a chaise lounge with blond, permed strands of hair hanging over it and a slim shoulder with a sore-looking pink stripe of sunburn. The girl was there, too, absently scratching her cheek beneath the awning as she watched him cycling toward them; she went around to the other side to meet him on the track.

She was wearing wide shorts with darts down the front and a sleeveless blouse knotted under her prominent belly button. Her bare feet with slender toes were planted wide apart in the gravel. Benoît stopped his bike beside her and let himself be kissed on both cheeks. One corner of the narrow slit of her mouth was raised again in that faintly sly little smile. Two brown shadows, like finger prints on either side of the bridge of her nose, made her appear to squint. In a way she looked like Vincent; she was so much less pretty than Louise, it was a sin.

She told him that her name was Cathy and that she was here with her aunt whose family lived in the area. Her derisive expression emphasized the foreign way she drawled out her words. Benoît wondered what she knew about them exactly. She asked when Vincent was coming back, but only for the sake of saying something, for she clearly knew the answer. Her eyes scanned his face, as though she was trying to remember something Vincent had said about him. Benoît felt aroused without any real reason: he did not like Cathy and he could not square her image with the memory of the obscenely open buttocks that had passed fleetingly through his mind. A long way off, the drone of the midday traffic streaming endlessly behind the house was amplified by the distance. Benoît found it weird to think he had had such an idyllic vision of their camp the whole time. Smoke from the barbecue was billowing over their side. Cathy suggested he stay to lunch; his refusal made her laugh. There was something off-putting about her, yet she caused Benoît the same feelings of mildly reprehensible complicity he experienced with Vincent. As he was getting back on his bike, she kissed him again on both cheeks and told him she had a girlfriend in town they could go out with when Vincent was back. Benoît set off again with the dizzying conviction that they were sufficiently dissolute to do it. He skirted the empty lot and rode in full view alongside the corn. His throat and lungs burnt with excitement, and he felt a thrill as he stamped on the pedals and shook himself. For the first time in ages, pleasure was unalloyed by guilt.

A dark green truck was sitting at the entrance to the parking lot; the man resting his elbow on the open window looked as though he had been cooling his heels for some time. Benoît walked past the front of the house to glance through the window: he was not expecting to see his father and he saw him now, sitting at the living room table opposite Louise, who sat very straight like a schoolgirl. It might have been his fifth visit in nine years. He still looked fit and handsome in an olive-skinned, nervous way. A gold medallion glinted in the open neck of his shirt and gave him a slightly disturbing appearance. He had come to fetch a hoist that had been left in the garage and was embarrassed and somehow out of step with the terrible news, which suddenly seemed already a thing of the past. Benoît could not understand how his mother could leave Louise on her own in such a situation. His father got up to shake his hand. He had the hesitant manner of someone caught in the act and looking for allies. Benoît noticed that the corner of one of his eyes was bloodshot; it gave him the frantic look of a bird. Louise and he must have been sitting in silence for some minutes already; she was trying to keep her hands over the scars not covered by her skirt. Benoît stood leaning against the doorframe, wanting just to avoid aggravating the awkwardness of this meeting, which was painful for Louise above all and which lasted long enough for the smell of lunch to reach them. His father had lit a cigarette and did not know where to stub it out when it came to kissing Louise. The little fleck of blood appeared to wander across his eye like a tear, and he was in fact upset. He followed Benoît into the corridor and was genuinely anxious to know if he might need the hoist. Before he left he had a brief conversation with their mother at the kitchen door. His tall, angular body jerked out the meaning of his words; possibly he was complaining that she had not told him or clumsily trying to ask how she was. Then he left at last after calling out a jovial goodbye across the living room.

Louise pouted when the truck was out of sight. The ordeal left her confused, distraught even at having burdened her father with so horrible a tragedy, with no attempt to soften the blow. Benoît thought her disturbingly generous. He put the TV on just to fill the silence that had descended again, and Louise sat down next to him on the sofa. She buried her lips in his blond hair, delicately extracting from it a tiny caterpillar that had rolled into a ball. He smelled of fresh air and raspberries. Lunch was ready; their mother came in to tell them to set the table and close the shutters against the scorching sun already creeping up to the garden fence. She was in a vindictive mood, the way she was whenever her ex-husband made an appearance. Yet in a way this unexpected visit had revived the sorrow of the first days after the death. Louise cried almost continually at lunch, but very calmly, leaning her head on her mother's shoulder, and for the first time she told her how guilty she felt. Benoît wondered how they could never have been bothered that Louise had said nothing up to now.

Vincent had called late in the evening to tell them he was coming the next day at about twelve. In the morning, Louise tidied her room and went to buy foundation to hide the scars on her thighs. She rallied a bit with something to look forward to and the need to get ready. She asked Benoît's advice about the foundation, apparently forgetful of the origin of her dreadful wounds. Her mother asked her several times to calm down; she was morose again, the way she had been when Vincent's arrival had opened old wounds. And in the course of that morning, while hundreds of frayed clouds floated through the sky over the house, the tension became palpable.

Vincent had washed the car and bought new red and black seat covers. Louise's greeting to him was surprisingly measured. Vincent took her into their room, probably to show her another bundle of bills, for she came down shortly afterward with a mysterious look of ingenuousness and confusion. Benoît did not like the strange atmosphere of these reunions. His mother, however, put up a brave front and showed no sign of the constant worry Louise's state caused her, but Vincent was on edge and the meal was spoiled by his restlessness. By two o'clock they had already finished eating. The weather was still overcast but heavy. Vincent grumbled that it was too hot; he wanted to go and look for CDs in S., and Benoît managed to persuade Louise to go with them.

Vincent had stopped talking of buying a motorbike and seemed, too, to want to take their minds off the idea, or at least preempt any questions on the subject by being exaggeratedly chatty and expansive. He seemed different to Benoît, and more determined, although he could not say about what. It was an odd, trying afternoon. They drove back to the sluggish rhythm of traffic jams. Louise struggled to breathe; she could not keep from touching the foundation, which was starting to resemble curdled milk on her scabs. Vincent still had not dared make any comment or even ask what she had been up to while he had been away; the radio blared increasingly loudly between them. Benoît's head ached; Louise would not stop turning around to him, as though to make up for the disappointment she, too, was starting to feel. They got back late, driving the last dozen miles in silence owing to the noise and heat. Louise's scars looked infected, but Vincent continued to ask no questions.

In the evening they had another fight in their room, but this time Vincent apparently did not insist, for he came down almost immediately to join Benoît in the garden. The dinner plates were piled up in the grass. Now and then a mosquito flew into the candle flame and went up in a puff of sputtering, smelly white smoke. In the distance, the sleeping caravan formed a pale splash against the shifting chiaroscuro of the woods. Vincent poured himself another glass of wine and signaled that they should wait, with a nod in the direction of the little bathroom window where a shadow was moving about. Benoît was intrigued as to what Vincent had to tell him and above all keen to see the awkwardness between them evaporate. The French window squealed briefly behind them: his mother was going up to bed and asked them to clear the dishes away, then she switched out the living room light and the silence was almost total. It was good; Vincent savored his wine and the suspense he was inflicting on Benoît. It was Sunday, and headlights from the steady stream of home-coming traffic swept over the empty lot within yards of the fence. Benoît said that he had met Cathy, and Vincent frowned impatiently, indicating that he knew. Being plunged back in the affluent atmosphere of his childhood had given him a kind of arrogance that jarred with their companionship. Benoît was sorry now that he had said anything about Cathy and pointlessly betrayed Louise. He started to stand up, but Vincent held on to his sleeve and pulled him back down.

He had fallen out with his parents. He spoke as though he did not care, but his eyes glistened. "They're mad at me for not having cried about the children. My father's gone crazy, he won't stop bawling and sobbing," he added, as though trying to convince himself. His cigarette shook between his lips, making little smoldering zigzags in the dark. When he had emptied his glass, Vincent said twice that you couldn't go on like that and Benoît did not know if he was talking about his father or himself. The hall light came on suddenly, and like an echo the caravan lantern brought a myriad of flickering shadows dancing over the lumpy ground of the empty lot. Someone flushed a toilet, and Vincent got up, gesturing to Benoît not to repeat what he had said. He stumbled slightly on his numbed legs and picked up a pile of plates to take them into the kitchen. Benoît followed with a dish and the breadbasket. He imagined, with a mixture of terror and admiration, that Vincent was preparing to go across to the caravan, but he found him filling the dishwasher, paying no more attention either to him or to what was going on outside. The glass in the bathroom door went black and a shadow moved across the top of the stairs. Vincent took a big lump of cheese, whose chalky texture stopped him talking for a moment. Benoît realized that they had finished off the bottle between them and must be a bit drunk. He was about to go out again when Vincent called to him over the banisters to say that, tomorrow or one of these days, he had something to tell him.

It was a bit before midnight. Benoît went back outside to put away the chaise lounges. A mosquito whined insistently in his ear but was not enough of a nuisance to make him want to go indoors. Louise's voice in the dark was like a cheerful little ghost. Benoît wanted to think the couple had made up, but this hope did not succeed in allaying the uncomfortable feeling Vincent had aroused with his confidences. His concern about the future for the three of them was becoming more defined. He comforted himself with the thought that school would soon be starting, investing this date with the power to produce some kind of miracle; he supposed that this might be what Vincent wanted to talk to him about.

All at once the caravan lights went out, turning the sky above the trees a strange steely grey. There were no more cars; the silence was unbroken, deep and smooth like a lake. Benoît was hot; his fears were finally starting to unwind with the alcohol.

Over the next few days Vincent appeared to have forgotten all about his schemes and irritations. August was drawing to a close, the heat was more bearable, the evenings shorter; the big houses were opening up again. Boredom and anxiety were becoming harder to combat, yet at the same time there was a growing sense of urgency. Louise reacted to this intangible pressure with the guileless smiles of a simpleton. Her wounds were beginning to heal over; with infinite patience she unstuck the scabs and took just as much pleasure watching the blood ooze as she did seeing the tender pink skin appear on her tanned legs. Vincent seemed more attached and attentive to her; his fight with his parents—he stubbornly refused to talk to them on the phone—was giving them another chance. Benoît wanted to think that Vincent had forgotten about Cathy.

The next Monday, his mother went back to work, and for a day the three of them found the monotony of their amusements broken by the fact of being on their own again. Vincent took them to the swimming pool. It was an exceptionally fine day. Louise leaned her head out of the window; tendrils of her hair scratched at the window right by Benoît's ear. The sun shone full on her face; she was scantily clad and wonderful.

They were the public baths where they often used to go with their father when they were small. Louise had a chilly memory of concrete changing rooms and voices echoing as though in a cave; she wanted to get changed in the car and asked them to stand in front of the windows so she would not be seen wriggling out of her skirt. The baths were full of children, whose cries scampered across to them from all over on the other side of the railings. Neither Benoît nor Vincent dared say anything, dreading suddenly the moment when Louise would notice the racket already so distant and almost forgotten. But Louise crossed the grass to the big pool without hearing the children, or at least without confusing them with images that must haunt her continually, and Benoît realized that he had no idea what it meant to mourn an absence day after day.

Benoît lay down beside her, straight on to the concrete slabs. She smelled of coconut; she was so close to him that he could read on her face the agonizing but pleasurable sensation of the scorching concrete on her belly. A strong smell of chlorine filled their nostrils and made them screw up their eyes. Vincent had gone to have a swim and he smiled at them through chattering teeth six feet away, his head level with the concrete. He swam another two laps before coming to join them. Louise laughed nervously at being dripped on as she felt him nearing her skin. Vincent's lips were blue. He placed his wet face against hers, and she kissed him with a long kiss that gave Benoît a hard-on. The smell of chemicals, sweat, and warm sun cream formed a heady mix. Lying between the two of them, Louise seemed to enjoy a sensual happiness that was unusual for her. Vincent's dark footprints faded as if by magic from the concrete, and gradually the heat grew heavy and enveloping.

Louise must have dozed off, for her smile turned into a pout that glistened with cocoa butter. A fine mist of sweat veiled her upper lip and the little dent in the curve of her back. Benoît was thirsty but his desire to move was checked by the pleasure of watching her, a pleasure that went back to his childhood. Vincent had lit a cigarette and was smoking it, leaning on his elbows. On the other side of the pool, where clutches of shivering kids were endlessly disappearing and popping up again, Benoît spotted Cathy eating a sandwich. She was sitting on a tiny towel beside the blow-up mattress where her aunt was reading. Benoît had the feeling that she and Vincent had been eyeing one another for a while already. Louise slumbered on, her body totally inert. On the other side, Cathy had finished her sandwich and was talking to her aunt without taking her eyes off them. This new, close confrontation was subject to the same rules as those imposed by the empty lot. Benoît tried to get Vincent's attention, but Vincent was completely absorbed by this silent exchange; the intensity was becoming almost palpable. Benoît glanced down to see if Louise was still asleep, and when he looked up, Cathy was tying her hair back, pushing her breasts out at Vincent, whom she appeared not to see now. Her olive-colored body was as lithe as a leopard's. Vincent had stubbed out his cigarette in the cap of a beer bottle and sat with his head hunched between his shoulders, watching Cathy through the strands of hair plastered to his head by his swim. Benoît was starting to get nervous. Beside him, Louise made a funny click with her tongue as she sought for air in her mouth which heat and sleep had parched, then she sighed and seemed to sink even flatter on the slab.

Cathy had dived into the water; they could just make out her blurry form crossing the pool from end to end. She emerged ten feet away in a great ripple, put her arms on the tiled edge, and leaned her dripping face on them. Her indifference toward them was convincing.

Cathy stayed several seconds facing them and ignoring them; against the light the pool's artificial blue brought out the mossy brown hue of her skin and gave it a curious sheen. Then, with not so much as a glance in their direction, she gave a backward lunge and vanished in a shower of water. Benoît lost sight of her among the sea of bathers. Vincent was starting to fidget but kept his face averted; they were probably both in the same state of arousal. Cathy had resurfaced on the other side of the pool. Her hair was dragged down in a long pointy tongue between her shoulder blades. She heaved herself out of the water in one bold move and was back leaning over her towel. Benoît thought again of a wiry, untouchable desert animal. His prick was hard beneath his belly. Vincent had traced an arrow on the concrete with the sharp end of a pebble; the drawing made them laugh.

When Benoît laid his cheek against the ground again, Louise was watching him with her blue, almost pupil-less eyes, and he had the disturbing feeling she had never taken her eyes off him or stopped sensing him in her sleep. However, she blew him a sleepy kiss, complaining mildly that the concrete was scratchy, then, without moving a muscle of her body, she turned her head to Vincent and offered him her lips. Her sweetness seemed to recall him from a journey miles away. He stared at her, as though at some forbidden marvel, and gave her a derisive smile with which Louise seemed bizarrely in league.

She was hot and sat up, spent some time brushing her hair, then rolled it on to her shoulder and approached the pool with feline caution. Benoît watched her buttocks flatten prettily as she sat for a moment on the mosaic edge of the pool before sliding noiselessly into the water. Her face appeared at practically the same spot where Cathy's had been five minutes before, and, probably to erase this memory, Vincent dived in right beside her. Benoît saw Louise dog paddle her way over to him and hang on to his neck as though clinging to a rock. He dived in himself. The water was cold but not enough to calm his excitement or fear at knowing Cathy so close. Thousands of oily eyes floated on the surface among the bees struggling not to be submerged at the concrete edge, where little waves repelled them time after time. Benoît swam a few laps to fight off a feeling of foreboding. Vincent and Louise swam not too far out, he swimming backward and she holding his hands, keeping her chin well out of the water like a swan. He was attentive to her and undoubtedly loved her at that moment as he seldom did.

Cathy had come down to the edge and was standing right over their heads, which she brushed several times with her animal-like foot. Benoît forced himself not to see her and even to push her out of his thoughts. But Cathy was not malicious, maybe just intrigued by this tragic, blond beauty whose sorrow must have struck her as a kind of phenomenon, for after giving Benoît a discreet wave she went back to her place beside her aunt and did not move again. Vincent let go of Louise's hands as though she was no longer at risk, and encouraged her to strike out toward the middle of the pool. Benoît joined them; Cathy's attitude had emboldened him, and he grabbed Vincent by the shoulders and dragged him down to the bottom where they wrestled for a moment to release their tension and desire. Louise's all but motionless body was drifting slightly, suspended by her chin on the surface. The pallor of her eyes merged with the rippling reflection of the water where her hair fanned out like a corolla. Louise could swim but she was sinking because nothing in her now thought of putting up a struggle. Vincent held her under the arms and brought her to the side, and she stood there bewildered for a few seconds, coughing in the water. She was not afraid, perhaps not even aware of her weakness.

That same day, at the end of the afternoon, Vincent took Benoît on his date with Cathy. Louise was in the shower when they left; she shouted to them to bring her back some chewing gum. They did not speak until the woods. Vincent was chewing a stalk of grass and kicking at the stray alfalfa flowers that had taken root in the dust. Both were red-eyed and still smelled of chlorine. Benoît did not know why Vincent had needed a witness, nor why he himself had so readily agreed. Perhaps they just wanted to give each other courage to be selfish and disgusting.

Cathy made no allusion to their meeting at the pool.

They followed her through the woods. Her bare feet in their rubber boots made a kissing sound; she beat the ferns down in front of her with a stick, flushing out pairs of black-birds, which pierced the leafy silence with their alarm calls. Vincent walked beside her a couple of paces away, hardly speaking to or touching her. Benoît was amazed at the tac-it assurance their relations had developed: it was no longer a question of fondling or sweet nothings between them. Cathy now seemed less brazen but already much more of a threat to Louise. Benoît was wanting her again, the way one wants not a body, but confidence in pleasure, and she must have noticed, for she began to laugh in Vincent's ear. They had reached the field beside the river; it was warm and golden. Benoît was aroused beyond endurance and raged silently at finding himself so intimidated. Seeing that he was lagging behind, Cathy turned back to fetch him. She pulled him by the hand to the hut then, half friendly, half derisive, she stuck her tongue in his mouth while Vincent took her from behind and started massaging her breasts. It was a full-mouthed kiss, and over Cathy's shoulder Ben-oît could see Vincent's bloodshot eyes following the con-scientious movement of mouths and tongues. Then he felt her hand working along his belt, slipping down between his legs over the little hollow at the base of his spine, fum-bling in the seat of his pants as though in a bag, and now nearly at his penis. Vincent still stood arched against her hips, giving great thrusts that unbalanced them, and Ben-oît suddenly felt Cathy's mouth spitting him out in a shout of wild laughter. Vincent's gesticulations had crushed them against the hut and Cathy was laughing out loud, trying to keep hold of Benoît's face, but he turned away, suddenly sober. Vincent did not immediately get annoyed and Benoît was too embarrassed to stay. He dived down toward the river and took refuge out of sight beneath an arch of wild roses and a tangle of catmint that formed a kind of nest. When he turned around he could make out Cathy sidling around the hut with Vincent in pursuit, the narrow shape of his penis sticking out of his pants at an angle. For a moment Benoît thought of going home without waiting for them, but this seemed even more disloyal than the betrayal to which he had just been accomplice. His erection was trapped in his underpants, which Cathy had twisted; he freed himself and came pretty quickly, relieving himself unashamedly of a desire for her that had been building up for days.

They were silent as they made their way back, retracing their steps through the woods. Evening was falling and the lapping of the water sounded more echoey and chilly. Cathy walked a few paces behind, more serious suddenly, even appearing to want to make it up with Benoît or at least be forgiven for laughing at him. There was no way of detesting her or of hating Vincent either, whose choice seemed somehow inevitable.

Louise was at her window when Benoît and Vincent emerged from the trees; she smiled at them the whole time it took them to cross the empty lot, while behind them Cathy lit a barbecue. The trees pushed out the thick, oily smoke around their feet. As they drew near the corner of the house, Vincent told Benoît that he was going off with Cathy in September. They had forgotten all about Louise's chewing gum.

More than a week had gone by since this rendezvous with Cathy, and the vaguely shameful memory of it had been dulled by other worries. They were in the last days of August. Benoît had stayed in bed, while the midmorning sun gnawed at the sheets; he felt as though a great weight was numbing his body. Louise was in S. for the day with an old school friend who had come to see her the day before. His mother must have gone out, Vincent probably, too. He had said nothing more about going off with Cathy and seemed busy with other things; the hope that he had changed his mind was marred by his irritability, and the whole thing was becoming slowly intolerable.

The phone began to ring—just a few rings, but strident, like a human cry, and Benoît eventually got up and went downstairs to make himself a coffee. The fridge stank of stale milk; on the windowsill, apricots were turning brown in a basket swarming with tiny flies. The breakfast things, probably left by Louise and Carine, were still on the table. Everything seemed grim and repulsive this morning; Benoît did not feel like anything. His mother had just come in; he heard the rustle of plastic bags in the hallway and was sorry he had not gone back up to his room.

She was made up and had bought a pair of beige sandals that made her plump flesh bulge over the straps. Benoît thought she looked tired. He poured her a coffee and she sat down at the end of the table and drank it with her face to the sun, which was already warm and veiling the windows. The sandals had left wide red marks on the bridge of her bare feet as they rested on the floor tiles. She wanted to know where Vincent was and why Benoît had not gone out; her eyes scanned his face a bit insistently.

"What have you done with all your girlfriends?"

She had taken hold of his arm to stop him from evading the question. The palm of her hand felt both padded and rough, her nails hard and not very pleasant against his skin. Benoît felt so depressed by the limitations of these holidays, by Vincent's aggressive mood over the past week, and by his own pointless scruples and laziness that he nearly shouted that he was on his own because Louise had ruined his life by being careless, but he just shrugged his shoulders and mumbled that his pals were on holiday. His mother pursed her lips in despair at his answer, but she did not insist. She let go of his arm and sank back in her chair, staring at the window. A myriad of little burst capillaries sparkled in her eyes, but Benoît did not care if he made her cry; he did not want to be involved in any feelings of anguish anymore. He asked what the time was, not to know but so that he could get up. His bitterness about Louise was mounting like a fever, causing him a kind of masochistic pleasure. It felt suddenly good to stop being fair or scrupulous, to stop excusing her sickly indolence, to stop loving her body that was growing unsightly with inaction. Tears choked Benoît and he felt a sort of rage in his belly. He gave up the idea of taking a shower and went out. His bike had been sitting in the sun and the saddle felt like a hot thigh between his legs; his unwashed body itched. He rode along the rackety little path that cut straight through the whispering corn; the hope that he might manage to find Vincent and Cathy filled him with wild energy.

But there did not seem to be anyone about at the caravan. The torn corner of the awning cracked like a whip, the radio was silent. Benoît leaned his bike against the caravan's rust-blistered side and pressed his face to the window. Cathy's aunt appeared in the dingy jumble of bunk beds; she beckoned to him to come in. She was with a girlfriend whom he felt he had seen before. The aunt introduced them—Benoît was amazed she knew his name—and took three beers out of the fridge. The space inside was minimal and so full of their washing and smells under the low ceiling that coming in felt like trespassing. Benoît was starting to wish he had not come, embarrassed by his own perspiration. The two women chatted to each other in a language he did not understand; Benoît could not have said if they were amused by his discomfort or by the situation, or else by what Cathy had maybe told them about him. They clearly knew nothing about the children's death, but they knew Vincent very well and sheltered his infidelities with the complacent bonhomie of cheated women for other people's husbands. There was a vulgarity about them and the same disenchanted familiarity with men and love that he found irksome in his mother but which impressed him in these women. They made him feel a sort of impunity with them, a pre-disaster virginity that filled him with nostalgia and made him want to cry.

They did not have much to say to one another; it was growing more and more awkward and arousing, being here while Cathy and Vincent were no doubt thrusting, in a tangle of penis and tongues, against the gnarled planks of the hut or on the backseat of the car. The two women were muscular and wiry, the tendons stood out in their necks when they crossed their arms. The beer and probably the unease of their silences made them laugh. The younger one had very fine eyes with too much makeup on and a thick mane of dyed auburn hair. Benoît desired her wide mouth, which promised to be extremely soft in the dry, tanned skin. She was leaning forward to hear the laconic answers he gave her questions; her fingers were covered in rings and clasped the beer can with the elegance of a smoker; the smell of cigarettes and a faint, sourish nighttime odor hung on her breath. Cathy's aunt had gone to hang out the wash, and for a few seconds, made fuzzy and tingling by the effects of alcohol, Benoît sat still and waited in an incredibly strong state of premonitory arousal for the woman to touch him. Yet, when she had rubbed her hands together to dry the moisture from the cold beer can, she merely pinched his knee to urge him to stand up. Cathy's aunt had come back and Benoît felt he was being dismissed from this life of fun whose frustration tortured him; he hated himself for blushing as he said good-bye.

He went straight to the hut. It was still cool under the trees; his T-shirt was damp with sweat and slapped icily around his hips. The roots caught on his laces and held up his bike. Benoît felt increasingly shaken by the emotions of this encounter, by the echo it had left in him and by the regrets it caused and which it seemed sweet to wallow in. He had reached the river. The hut was empty and as stifling as an oven under its tarpaulin roof now laced all over with a pattern of silver-glistening snail trails. All around, the wind stirred the fields with a sound like people walking about. Benoît felt too tense to wait; he went down to the road to see who was fishing there that morning. But the cars parked at the roadside meant nothing to him. It was past midday; Louise was bound to have returned. Benoît felt no anger now and no bitterness, just pity at the sense of his love for her and of the tragedy for them both.

A car was parked outside the house, but the shutters to Louise's room were closed and everything led him to suppose that she was lying up there, her body collapsed in the sleep of amnesia. Light from the garden revealed his mother and Carine in the end room. He had not closed the door properly: a warm draft blew a window shut with a bang that made both women turn. Benoît ran upstairs; his mother's step followed quietly to the bottom but went no further. The artificial gloom of a household sleeping late filled the corridor. Benoît tiptoed into Louise's room. Summer blazed like glowing embers on the slatted shutters. Despite the light breeze, the heat was insufferable. Louise lay on her back, snoring gently. She was in her underwear and her chest and belly were running with sweat. The white foam Benoît knew only too well looked like speech marks opening at either corner of her full lips; he felt as though he was looking at someone washed up, covered in salt and sand and beyond help.

His mother was waiting for him downstairs by the living room door. She cut short his complaints and explained that Louise had had a burst of hysterics in a shop and had had to be brought straight back. Her mouth was pinched unpleasantly—perhaps she was just cross at being deprived of having a Saturday to herself. Pity was already giving way to lassitude. She had too much energy to sympathize beyond what was bearable. Carine's embarrassed carefulness even suggested that she had confided to her that she had lost hope and that, like Benoît, she, too, sometimes let herself think that Louise might not have met with such bad luck if she had been more grown-up and responsible. It had become somehow inevitable and acceptable to put up defenses against her misery; such, at least, was their only excuse.

Carine had taken herself off to a corner of the garden. Benoît's memories of her were full of jealousy. She had always worked harder at school than Louise and she used this throughout their childhood as though exercising a right to be cruel, making her go over her homework and deciding what games to play when she came to stay at the house. Louise was conscientious and docile with her, constantly coming within an inch of betraying Benoît and punishing herself. Their friendship was a kind of torture but Louise nevertheless remained loyal to it until she met Vincent. Benoît suspected that Carine must have made her cry by believing herself able and entitled to shake her out of her grief. He went up to his room without greeting her, pleased to be on the same side as Louise.

Benoît had not heard Vincent come in and it was Louise's laughter that alerted him to his presence. He went out on to the landing. The bedroom door and window were wide open; little patches of sunlight flickered on the walls. She was putting on a skirt, hanging on to Vincent's shoulder. Her own weakness made her laugh; she flopped against his chest without the strength to do up the straps of her sandals. Vincent was stroking her neck, resting his chin on the top of her head as though on an altar. She gave a wonderful smile when she saw Benoît at the door. It was nearly two o'clock; Carine was still downstairs with their mother. Her grating voice carried through the house. Louise hid her face in Vincent's shirt so as not to hear her. She was funny like this, almost merry, and Benoît told himself with relief that he still loved her. Her parched lips were stained with a thin trickle of blood, and Benoît also noticed strands of saliva in her mouth when she asked Vincent to close the window, as if cracks were starting to appear in her beauty. But there were still her incredible kindness and the absolute trust she had in them. They constituted a sort of gift that sometimes touched on grace. Benoît thought she was enjoying something approaching peace, clasped between them like this, and that, if they could just be generous enough, loving her so simply might be, for them too, an acceptable and, when all was said and done, a cheerful form of happiness.

III

B ut the holidays were drawing to a close, and the remaining time left little room for pity. Vincent had gotten involved in a vague scheme for a radio business with an old friend from S., apparently glimpsing a possible way out of his prevarications in secrecy and wheeler-dealing. Louise was now left to drift more on her own. Benoît was no more capable than Vincent of filling the gulfs opening up in her; his energy was incompatible with the unhealthy siestas that immobilized Louise and the house in the heat of the afternoon. The caravan had been shut up for several days; there was no more amusement to be had from that quarter anymore either. Summer was nearly over, sultry and crackling over the region. At night, rain washed and swelled the river waters, and they watched it plunging along beneath the wild roses, where ripe scarlet berries had replaced the flowers. Louise listened to Benoît talk of going swimming; her eyes followed him like an acrobat, but her body shrank at the thought of the cold water and of going all that way, or just simply at the intangible distress of leaving the house. And Benoît could neither bring himself to go out anyway nor forgive her completely for holding him back. Their mother was at work, and Vincent went out early and only occasionally called in in the afternoon. Benoît remained alone with Louise, sometimes for whole days. Fog now obliged them to close the windows in the morning, and the silence of the pair of them hung heavy in the rooms, as implacable and depressing as the recent August heat. Benoît killed time as best he could, spending a lot of it in mounting an old motorbike engine onto the sidecar. Sometimes Louise would come and keep him company, seated on a trunk with shoulders hunched and her legs crossed under the brief skirts she wore, shivering in spite of the heat under the metal sheeting that made her face smooth with sweat; at these times, their affection was equal and almost happy. But mostly she hung back, as though no longer sure of Benoît's love. She seldom went out, living by Vincent's timetable out of habit or kindness, and her sporadic tidying sprees were not enough now to keep her alive. Benoît one day saw her drop a dish although she was holding it in both hands, quite simply because her strength was starting to wane. She had pulled an almost comical face of regret to limit not the damage, but her own decline, and Benoît had gone up to his room to weep. Their mother had just come home and she exchanged sharp words with Louise, then she went up to find Benoît, pulled his head out of the pillows, and begged him furiously not to get upset. In that moment, the violence of her grasp had done him good, as had the fact that she had for once shown so clearly what she wanted. Her face was ugly, flabby with the weight she had put on, but dramatic with feeling; tiny burst veins like little stars showed through what was left of her makeup after a morning's work. Benoît suddenly realized the full extent of the havoc events had wrought in her and how hard she had fought to hide this from them. She got up to wipe her eyes in the reflection of the windows; before she went out, she promised that she had found the answer for Louise when term began, and for an instant Benoît had the desperate, cowardly hope that she had thought of a means of sending her away.

Another two days passed while Benoît tried to deal with the hope his mother's promise had inspired. It was a Tuesday, and she had the day off; she was having lunch in town, and came back at about two, together with a young woman who ran a crockery store in town. They had coffee in the garden, shielded by the empty lot from the dusty cornfields, where harvesting had been shredding the plants since morning. Their lively conversation created an unusual atmosphere, and Louise must have felt excluded or hurt by it, for she took a long time coming downstairs. She had put on a white linen dress that was out of keeping with the place and occasion, and she looked both tragic and irritating. Benoît did not go back to the garage straightaway. She made a funny noise in her throat, as though she was choking on her own saliva, then put her hands flat down on her knees and sat staring into the distance, her painted lips sealed in an impassive pout. The woman smiled now at Benoît, now at his mother, perhaps trying to preempt their displeasure or disappointment. Benoît felt like shouting at Louise to stop it. Flocks of birds had been gathering in the sky since morning, and they added to the strange tension of the moment.

The idea was that Louise would work a few days a week at the shop, and this she had had no trouble guessing, for she remained unmoved. The woman drew her chair closer to explain how this would suit both of them; she was pleasant and flirtatious, with imitation gold at her wrists that cast sparkles over Louise's face as she listened, narrowing her eyes. Benoît thought for a moment that she was going to yield to the woman's friendliness, but when she stopped talking, Louise turned away slightly and replied that she did not have to work because her husband had lots of money. Benoît wondered what planet she thought she was on. It would have been easy to see that Louise was clinging to the memory of a dream of happiness with Vincent because she could not create a new life for herself; but they were no longer capable of such compassion. Benoît was flabbergasted. His mother stood up to pick up a sock that was trailing in the grass and merely asked Louise to go up to her room in a voice that showed that, from now on, she was washing her hands of the business. So Louise put the cups she and the woman had used on a tray, dramatically swept her hair back, and went in. There was something reckless about her defiance, arrogant and fragile at the same time, and she persisted to the point of playing the radio loud enough for it to be heard in the garden. Benoît would have liked to go and join her, but he was far too depressed and no longer sure enough of his loyalty to his sister. The plunder of the cornfields had started up again under the eyes of the wheeling birds; the whole area was a mass of smoke, and Louise closed her shutters. Nothing more was said by any of them. The woman had silenced the rattle of her bracelets with a hand and was staring at the straggle of birdsfoot trefoil by the fence. She cannot have expected a disaster like this, and indeed, they now seemed able to do themselves nothing but harm.

Louise retreated into silence till evening. Toward six, Benoît saw her steal her mother's little makeup pouch and disappear into her bedroom. She had left on her white dress and was doubtless getting ready in the hopes of an outing with Vincent, which would somehow prove her right against them. Her mother had gone to take the woman back and did not return. Benoît dared not leave Louise on her own. Their sulkiness weighed on him. He went up on to the landing several times, hoping she would sense his presence and his unhappiness by his hushed manner, but Louise stayed barricaded in, determined to believe that she had been abandoned. She was relying on Vincent's love, and Benoît was astonished how gullible she could be and began to dread another scene. Vincent, however, came home early and in a good mood that day. He was touchy about money and immediately rallied to Louise's hurt feelings. Benoît heard them murmuring in the bed-room, and then the bed creaking, but so quietly that he wanted to cry. Later, he saw them dash out to the car with their arms around each other as though hurrying through a downpour. Louise's face was transformed; her exaltation made him fear the worst.

It was past eight o'clock; the car windows blazed in the setting sun and Louise's dress looked pink. Vincent kept hold of her hand; he must have been sufficiently affect-ed to think he was still capable of loving her. The wind showered the car with gravel and sang around the high steel streetlamps along the main road. Vincent did not start the engine. Benoît could see Louise's bare thighs and her mouth, unusually voluble, reflected in the rearview mirror. What was she saying to him and what promises was he making? Benoît wondered how his mother could have been so thoughtless as to push Louise into this new madness.

He was woken up late that night by Louise's weight on the edge of the mattress. Light from the bedside lamp looked fuzzy through his moist eyes. She was smiling. She put her soft mouth to his and hugged him awkwardly, con-stricted in the tight dress, which cramped her effusions. A ray of light appeared under the door; Louise switched off the light and was silent. Benoît could only just sense her breathing; he felt the heat from the white oblong of her armpit against his forehead and made out the line of her hips in the weak glimmer from the landing. They stayed clinging together until their mother had gone back to bed, the way they had done when they were children and Louise used to come and dream aloud of slushy love stories from TV serials. Then, in a reedy voice that smelled of lemonade, she told him that Vincent was going to take her far away. She looked at him with infinite longing as if she were saying, please and I'm sorry.

Probably Vincent had been sincere, but the truth at that time was quite different. It must have been the following Friday. Since the day before, a midsummer heat had held the world in suspense of a storm. Louise had already sobered up from Vincent's promise; she woke up feeling nauseous at midday, her breath acid and her eyelashes stuck together. Vincent ran her a cool bath and she got in as timidly as an invalid. He wiped a wet flannel over her face—Benoît saw her hunch over as though such gentleness was torture to her—then he kissed her and went out, quietly shutting the bathroom door, and she stayed making the lapping water echo around the tiled room. Benoît was mending the transistor radio in the kitchen, Vincent was on the phone. When he tried to go to the bathroom, he found the door locked. He tapped several times, but Louise made no answer. Vincent had just hung up; the unlikelihood of this silence seemed very slowly to strike him, too, and it was the mesmerized expression on his face that made Benoît think that they were both imagining she was dead.

They stood for a few seconds listening to the faucet dripping into the bathwater. It was now Vincent's turn to knock at the door, but the silence persisted; it was a bit surreal. Benoît had made no move; he wondered how long they could stand there staring at each other, doing nothing. Then there was a violent screech of brakes outside that brought the harsh reality of what they were thinking abruptly to the fore. They rushed into the garden. The sun on the house walls was dazzling, the fields were still and totally devoid of any sign of life. Benoît climbed over the fence, which creaked under his weight. He had grazed the inside of his leg, and Louise watched him curse and double up in pain; she must have thought she was a bit to blame because she launched into an explanation of how she had gotten out of a window to pick up an earring that had fallen into the thick nest of brambles down beside the wall. Tiny beads of blood appeared on her arm where she had scratched it as she withdrew it hurriedly from the thorns. Vincent tucked it behind her back as though to shield her from the images he had had in his mind the whole time. Seeing them behaving so oddly, Louise took a step back and straightened her bra under her top. Benoît did not know where to look, dazed by the traffic streaming past the house with a noise like a human scream. He made a show of hunting among the brambles, but Louise told him not to worry, they were just trinkets she had bought at the drugstore. Then she added that she was not even sure she had lost it here, and also that she would never manage to get back in through the window. She seemed to be feeling blindly for an answer to their strange behavior. Her wet hair made damp patches on her vest-top, her face looked somehow strangled by the clinging strands. Vincent told her she would catch cold and walked back along the front of the house with her while Benoît climbed in through the window to go and unlock the door.

Louise had not dared go back to her old sleepy habits after this, while for their part they did not dare go out immediately. She made them something to eat and went to the effort of talking and smiling. The shorn fields where birds fussed and twittered seemed to stretch the profound hush of that day as far as the eye could see. In spite of the fine weather, Louise did not put out the sun lounges. Vincent and Benoît's boredom must have mirrored the image of her own idleness, for she appeared to find the time even more difficult than they. Finding them skulking in the living room on such a sunny day, their mother set about finding them something to do with unusual bossiness. It was the most dismal afternoon the three of them had ever spent together; and it was probably the impossibility of being happy together, parching their mouths like thirst, coupled with the fear of having been capable of imagining her suicide earlier on, that tipped the balance of Vincent's decision.

Benoît watched TV till quite late that evening. At about one o'clock, not long after he had gone to bed, he heard the crunch of steps on the parking lot then a creaking along the landing. At the time, it did not even occur to him that Vincent might have gone to find Cathy.

Benoît got up early the next morning to finish mounting the engine onto the sidecar. Vincent came to find him at about eleven. The garage was full of fumes and like an oven, though the shadow from the house had reduced the heat by a few degrees; the echo of the first revolutions still floated in the air. Vincent had brought some beers with him partly as an excuse to have a chat. They both felt bad about what had happened the day before and were looking for a kind of absolution in each other that created a helpful atmosphere of mutual tolerance. Gradually, the prospect of trying out the sidecar had the effect of dispelling the rotten images weighing on their minds.

Just as they were pushing the sidecar to the door, Benoît noticed a stationary sedan at the entrance to the parking lot. The face of the man sitting beside his mother was blanked out behind the dazzling, insect-spattered windscreen. Benoît shrank back out of the light, wanting to see her no more than he wished to hear Vincent's remarks. Vincent, however, was silent and even seemed curiously informed about what was going on. Shadows and straw dust whirled about the empty road in the breeze. Benoît had finished his beer, his ears were buzzing; having to wait was making him nervous. The shadow of the car spread right to the corner of the parking lot. Benoît saw the door open; he heard his mother thanking someone repeatedly before hurrying into the house. Their presence, or the blackness of the open garage, made her stumble, and she came to the entrance to ask what the two of them were up to. Benoît noticed that she was hiding an envelope in her hand and had not changed her clothes; he thought she looked oddly flustered. Behind her, the car park was suddenly plunged in darkness. The weather was clouding over; it was nearly one o'clock. Benoît wanted his mother to go away so he could try out the sidecar before lunch, and she guessed this immediately for she went in with a curious sweep of her arm as though gathering a shawl about her shoulders. Before she disappeared, she made him promise not to take the contraption onto the road.

The engine shuddered into life again at the first attempt, like a plane. Benoît was staggered by its power and filled with a kind of nervous hilarity. He told Vincent to get on the back and drove onto the dirt road still littered with shreds of corn leaves. The handlebars shook and sent jolts right through him; gusts of fresh air from the trees swept into their faces. Benoît felt like yelling with happiness. Behind him, Vincent sat more and more stiff and withdrawn, probably afraid of their bodies touching. Benoît could hear his breath coming loudly through his nose, now and again with a catch in it when they went over a bump; they must both have been in the same state of intense exhilaration.

They found Cathy shaking out a rug into the bushes near the reservoir. She had pinned her hair up and was wearing yellow rubber gloves that emphasized her slim arms. Benoît suddenly realized that she had started tidying up the caravan with a view to leaving and that Vincent knew this. The engine throbbed gently beneath him and in his chest; it was sweet and terrible. Cathy did not come toward them immediately, hampered as much by her carpet as by Benoît's presence. Vincent had not even said hello to her; he was barely resting his weight on the saddle now, and

Benoît switched off the engine to encourage him to get off, terrified he would start to cry in front of them.

Vincent had said he would only be a few seconds. Benoît watched him disappear among the trees with Cathy. He could think of nothing except not crying. Dry mustard stalks bristled over the empty lot and were blowing about in the wind. Louise had not yet got up; her closed shutters broke the symmetry of the housefront. Benoît wondered if it was possible that she still did not suspect anything. Directly behind him, the red splash of Cathy's blouse was disappearing among the green bushes. Vincent had just jumped onto the path; he was walking with his eyes on the house, clearly embarrassed by Benoît's disillusionment. The sidecar engine filled the woods with fumes and Benoît coughed slightly to swallow his tears. Vincent suggested driving into town, but Benoît's despair was too great to disobey his mother.

Louise had already gotten up when Benoît came downstairs the following morning. The weather was cooler still, and she was wearing one of Vincent's big, rough sweaters as a dress that made her legs look interminably long. When he woke up, Benoît had been filled with the certainty that Vincent was leaving; there was a sour taste on his tongue and he was annoyed with Louise for appearing happy. In the distance, under the trees swaying dangerously in the wind, a gray car was backing up to the caravan, already denuded of its awning. Benoît saw the woman with auburn hair get out, then Cathy's aunt, who stood bending into the gaping jaws of the trunk. The cheerful, busy atmosphere of leave-taking made him jealous. Vincent watched from the French window, looking as disoriented as the day before. Forcing himself not to look at the caravan was giving him nervous twitches. Louise had come and nestled against his arm to show off the orange nail polish on her short nails. She seemed oddly impervious this morning to his taciturn mood. Benoît could not help thinking that she was to blame for this departure and that he would end up hating her if he continued to be deprived of enjoyment much longer. His mother was cooking a roast; the smile of annoyance she gave his dejection, added to the greasy Sunday smells, only exacerbated his bitterness.

The car out there made a few more maneuvers, and the caravan trundled jerkily, lurching a few yards over the grassy hummocks of the track. Vincent would not stop running a hand through his hair, so that eventually Louise noticed this odd fact: their view was suddenly moving off after nearly two months of immobility. Fat clouds were building up over S., and the landscape was gradually sinking into shadow. The caravan came to a standstill. Vincent went to get himself a coffee; Benoît was choked with tears.

They had eaten without appetite and almost without speaking. Yet the temperature was balmy and the wind heavy with a strong smell of earth and storms, of gunflint. It was the last Sunday before term began and calmer than the others; the few cars looked crushed under their weight of luggage. Benoît thought that Elodie must be home and that he would have her botched caresses to make up for Vincent going. His mother observed his tearful eyes with an encouraging insistence that made him want to scream. The wind had dropped but the sky continued to fill with darkness. Louise pushed her chair back to take off her sandals. She contemplated the caravan for a moment, sucking at a peach, and asked suddenly if it was possible that they had electricity. As no one answered, she rested her bare feet on the edge of the chair and leaned against Vincent's shoulder. And, probably because he preferred (or wanted) to risk seeing the caravan leave without him rather than stay and watch from the house, Vincent suggested going to buy some more earrings at the drugstore along the freeway. Louise ran to get her bag; Vincent and Benoît waited for her in the car in the heat of the last ray of sun. They still had not said anything to one another since the morning; Benoît could hardly breathe, unable even to bring himself to ask when and how Vincent expected to make his getaway.

Vincent drove fast—Benoît supposed that he was bound to take the car with him, gradually realizing the limitations and silence his departure would mean. Louise was fiddling with the one forlorn earring, which she had slipped over a finger; seeing her in her own world made everything even more soul-destroying. They had now driven into the gray zone of clouds. Louise put her sweater back on and smiled at Benoît in the rearview mirror, and it was then that she must have noticed that something was wrong. She rested her cheek against the seatback and gave him a frowning little pout, forcing herself to appear cheerful but clearly dreading any new letdown with the instinct of a little animal. Benoît took the hand she held out to him but showed her only clumsy affection in the sense of frustration that had been gnawing at him since morning. She asked him if the sidecar was going well, and when he grudgingly said that it was, she sat back facing the road with a deep sigh. Benoît saw her lashes beating quicker and quicker and her hand drop the earring in the lap of her skirt. Vincent was not looking at her, but his impatience suggested that he, too, had noticed that she was about to cry. He decided that the weather was too threatening to go on and made an abrupt U-turn in the middle of the road. Louise watched him through the hair cradling her face, then she sank a bit lower in her seat but slowly, as though her whole body was falling apart. The worst of the storm was now behind them, together with the hill above the gravel pit where the oak trees merged with the chaos of clouds. Vincent remarked that they had had a lucky escape, but no one answered. Louise was now completely still in her seat.

The first flash struck the hill the moment they drew up in front of the house, and almost immediately huge drops began to splash against the windscreen. Louise huddled in her seat; in a few brief seconds the storm had closed in on them like a wall. Upstairs, the windows had been left open and swung to and fro in the darkened rooms. Louise half-opened the car door but shut it again immediately, surprised at the violence outside. Vincent then told her to wait and ran to the house with Benoît.

At the door, Vincent hesitated for a moment—Louise had completely disappeared from view behind the teeming rain, which all but hid the car. He lit a cigarette and it trembled between his lips, then, without taking his eyes off the car, he asked Benoît to go and see if the caravan was still there. Benoît hated himself for obeying but he, too, needed to know. He ran into the kitchen. The caravan had not moved and stood at the end of its mooring in the storm, which was already easing off. Its little windows were like pale yellow lights in the gloom; there was something cheerful about this chilly delay. Benoît drank a glass of orange juice to try to wash down his nausea; the injustice of this departure cut him to the quick. Vincent's voice made him jump; he had come to see what he was up to. A ray of sunlight fell on them between the last few drops of the cloudburst, and it was just as Louise was running to the door that Vincent suggested Benoît leave with him.

It was dark in the hallway; Louise appeared transfixed, magnificent. Her dripping hair clung about her like a cloth; she gave a puzzled little laugh when she caught sight of the two of them standing silent at the end of the corridor. Vincent wiped the spots of rain from her face, then drew his head back a fraction to get a better look at her, and Louise had to stand on tiptoe to reach his lips. She was hardly breathing and stood hugging him until he put his arms around her. Her anxiety was mounting with infinite caution, like a wordless appeal for mercy. She demanded nothing now, she just wanted to be comforted—and she was, Benoît too, in a sense. He was so tempted by Vincent's suggestion that he still preferred to hope that the whole thing would come to nothing.

His mother had been roused from her idleness by the storm and was sitting with her bare feet tucked under her, watching the rain pouring down over the caravan. She seemed surprised to find them back already and made room for Benoît on the sofa, then sat staring at him. Louise had gone to fetch towels and a hairdryer from the bathroom. She still had not noticed the caravan standing among the puddles on the dirt road as though it had broken down. Her extraordinary trust in Vincent had once more warmed and soothed her. Vincent watched her carefully unwind the hairdryer cord and plug it in. He let her do his hair, apparently finally conscious that he was going away and now reconciled to the idea. Benoît went into the kitchen to cut a slice of bread, the crazy idea of abandoning Louise echoing in him as though in a cave.

"Go with him." His mother had spoken so quietly that Benoît did not know if he ought to understand. The bread's soft dough made a warm, salty mound against the roof of his mouth, the whirr of the hairdryer seemed to distance Louise. His mother had started emptying the dishwasher; blood rushed to her face as she bent down. Again, she told him to leave and said that Vincent was okay about it and that she would give him money, the whole time without looking at him, as if he of all people should not be affected by the bitterness of her decision. Benoît wanted to deny that he had thought of it before, but his voice sounded funny to him and his mother silenced him by handing him a pile of plates. Louise came to replace the hairdryer. There was a tragic grace about her adolescent figure as she stood in the hall, which another shower was darkening. Benoît could see she was not totally easy and above all that what she was afraid of fell far short of the mark, but he could no longer suffer for her now, concerned only with his own nervousness and his fear that Vincent would change his mind.

It was nearly two o'clock when Benoît managed to steal away to collect his things. He felt as though he was obeying circumstances that were taking place outside himself and, as on the day of the accident, he was amazed at the bewildering suddenness with which one could go from one life to another. His mother and Louise were talking downstairs in the kitchen. Outside, the sky was clearing over the buildings in S., which stood out gilt-edged against the blueness. Benoît was aware only of his joy and distress. When he went down into the living room, Vincent was watching TV and Louise was standing by the sofa eating an apple. She gnawed the core for a long time before putting it in an ashtray, then she went over to Vincent, took his face in her hands and pressed it against her belly. She stood like this without moving, staring out of the window at the drenched chaise lounges and the sun-dappled caravan — Vincent had not dared put his arms around her hips, and Benoît saw that he had not closed his eyes, either.

She had spent another good hour beside Vincent in front of the TV; it seemed impossible to get away, unthinkable even that things could be other than they were. The caravan had not moved; a chair had been taken out of the trunk, but there was nobody about. The weather was beautiful, the world outside quivered in the sparkling droplets. Benoît let himself be lulled by the scene and by his own melancholy. Louise had gone upstairs to lie down; he had not even seen her go out of the room. The idea of going away struck him suddenly in all its craziness, and Vincent clearly felt it, too, for he sat on the edge of the sofa, rubbing his hands, glued to the TV. Louise's shutters clattered together. Her mother appeared at the banisters and signaled to them to hurry up; Benoît did not even want to think what she might have given Louise. He ran to get his bag from his room while Vincent took his from the cupboard under the stairs. Happiness was starting to fill him, flooding through him with the smart of sensual pleasure. His mother was hovering at the foot of the stairs holding an envelope; when he came down, she stuffed it into Benoît's pocket. He thought he had heard a cry but she motioned to him again to be quiet and get a move on. She was ageless, expressionless, perhaps finding the delay unbearable or else paralyzed at seeing her son finally running away like this. Benoît could not think how to say good-bye anymore; he did not like the feel of her cheeks but could not imagine leaving without kissing her. Vincent was already nearly at the empty lot, standing a bit impatiently with his knees slightly bent as though he had a stomach ache. The wind blew fat, slanting drops onto the gray parking lot. Then something banged upstairs, and Benoît blushed. His mother pushed him toward the door. Her siesta had rumpled her perm and her face sprang to life again as soon as he was outside, and the next time he turned around she had closed the door. He suddenly wanted to laugh at the crazy scheme they were involved in. Vincent was running ahead, his bag bumping against his shoulder. Rain lashed their cheeks and arms. Benoît had to stop to get his breath. Vincent was waiting for him a bit further on, unable to stay still or speak without raising his voice. Cathy had come out of the caravan and was walking toward them holding her hair against her ears; she was as excited as they and almost pretty.

Benoît waited for the car to start before he took the envelope out of his pocket. It was a cheque for twenty thousand francs signed by a hand he did not recognize; he wondered how his mother had managed to get hold of so much money.